T0355865

To Go On Living

Narine Abgaryan

To Go On
Living
STORIES

Translated by Margarit Ordukhanyan and Zara Torlone

Plough

Published by Plough Publishing House
Walden, New York
Robertsbridge, England
Elsmore, Australia
www.plough.com

ISBN 978-163608-152-6
29 28 27 26 25   1 2 3 4 5

Originally published in Russian as Дальше жить.
Copyright © 2021 by Narine Abgaryan.

This translation published by arrangement with the author
and Banke, Goumen, Smirnova Literary Agency.

English translation copyright © 2025 by
Margarit Ordukhanyan and Zara Torlone.

Cover art by Maretta Aivazian.

A catalog record for this book is available from the British Library.
Library of Congress Cataloging-in-Publication Data

Names: Abgaryan, Narine, author. | Ordukhanyan, Margarit Tadevosyan,
    translator. | Torlone, Zara M., translator.
Title: To go on living : stories / Narine Abgaryan ; translated by Margarit
    Ordukhanyan and Zara Torlone
Other titles: Dal'she zhit'. English
Description: Walden, New York : Plough Publishing House, 2025. | Summary:
    "Set in rural Armenia in the aftermath of war, these heartwarming short
    stories show people finding hope and purpose again"-- Provided by
    publisher.
Identifiers: LCCN 2024035677 (print) | LCCN 2024035678 (ebook) | ISBN
    9781636081526 (hardcover) | ISBN 9781636081533 (epub)
Subjects: LCGFT: Short stories.
Classification: LCC PG3491.3.B48 D3513 2025 (print) | LCC PG3491.3.B48
    (ebook) | DDC 891.73/5--dc23/eng/20240805
LC record available at https://lccn.loc.gov/2024035677
LC ebook record available at https://lccn.loc.gov/2024035678

Printed in the United States of America

Contents

In Place of a Preface
Zanazan

———————

"Zanazan! Hey, Zanazan! Would you like a pear?"

Zanazan has long eyelashes and lilac eyes. Her hair is thick, the color of copper, with no hint of gray. It curls into unruly ringlets by the temples.

I offer her the pear. She looks through it, her gaze fixed.

"Go ahead, take the pear, Zanazan."

She shakes her head no.

Zanazan's skin is olive-colored, with a dusting of red freckles. She is one of a kind, there's nobody else like her.

"Would you like anything?"

She covers her mouth with the back of her hand; the lifeline on her palm is smudged and short, broken at the midpoint.

"Zanazan?"

"Hm?"

"Talk to me."

She says nothing. Her fingers are long and pale, a simple ring on her left index finger. She has a funny way of standing, one leg crossed over the other. There is a half-moon-shaped scratch on her ankle.

"When did this happen?"

She shrugs and smiles vaguely, as if to herself.

I am aching to put my arms around her and press her to my chest, but I can't. Zanazan doesn't like to be touched.

"I'd draw you if I knew how."

She eyes me distrustfully and, after some hesitation, accepts the pear.

"Tell me something, Zanazan!"

She walks away, carefully shutting the door behind her.

In my mind's eye, I follow her down the stairs, one flight, then the next. She ducks out of the building's chill into the sun-drenched yard.

"Zanazan! Hey, Zanazan!" call out the kids.

She walks on without looking back. Her braid is tossed over her shoulder, held at the tip by a silly elastic band.

The war found Zanazan pregnant. She went into labor in the middle of an air raid. There was no calling an ambulance—the phone lines were dead. Going to the neighbors for help wouldn't do either—why ask people to risk their own lives? She held out for as long as she could. When the pain became too much to handle, she and her husband packed up and headed to the hospital. Her husband was mowed down by shrapnel; they were unable to save her child.

"Zanazan! Hey, Zanazan!" call out the kids.

She walks on without looking back.

She lives alone with her frail mother-in-law.

"Who's going to look after you when I'm gone?" frets her mother-in-law.

Zanazan smiles meekly and serenely as she hands the pear to her mother-in-law.

"Mm-mm-m."

She has thick, long lashes and lilac-colored eyes. Have you ever seen lilac-colored eyes? I have—Zanazan's.

Merelots

Ginamants[1] Metaksia leaves her house bright and early, at the crack of dawn. A flock of village swallows, having abandoned their perches in the cypress trees, are swooping overhead, making notches on the canvas of the quickly brightening sky with their sharp-tipped wings. The first dew—dense, life-giving—falls, dispatching the night. A cricket, confused about the hour of the day, breaks into its drawling song: chirr-up, chirr-up, chirr-up.

"Good morning to you too, you poor soul," Metaksia greets him in her mind. The cricket, as if hearing her thoughts, cuts off and falls silent.

Today is Merelots, the day of the dead. Traditionally, people attend the memorial service first and only after that visit the graves of their departed loved ones. There was a time when Metaksia also followed this tradition, but then she decided that it was not right to delay the visit to the dead—after all, what use do the departed have for liturgy when they have gone to a place where nothing worldly matters? Therefore, she figured, the proper way to go about it was to start the day of remembrance

---

1 A note about the names here and throughout the book. The first part of the two-word name of each story's protagonist is neither the given name nor the surname; rather, it is a collective family nickname bestowed upon each family by the local residents. It usually derives from a particular characteristic of each family's progenitor, although in other cases it may simply include that forebear's first name, plus a suffix, which, in the distinct regional dialect of Armenian spoken in Berd, is *-ants*.

with a trip to the graveyard before attending to any other business. So as to completely dispel any doubts, she consulted the priest. He heard her out and nodded in agreement: "You do what you think is right; if you feel more at peace doing things in this order, then you should." Metaksia certainly felt more at peace doing things in this order.

The cemetery is a ways off. The road that leads to it, paved with river stones, snakes between the houses and then, turning abruptly, climbs up the side of the hill, where the final resting places of the people of Berd keep multiplying, crowded against each other with their low fences. It's as if the people are trying to outdo each other in dying. It seems that only yesterday Razmik's grave was the one at the very end, but now you have to make your way past three rows just to get to it. Metaksia had picked a spot for him with plenty of room and plenty of open sky. She asked them to put him on the right side, in the shadow of the weeping willow. When her time comes, they'll put her on the left side; she's already made arrangements and even paid Tsatur, the gravedigger. Tsatur tried to turn down her money, but she insisted: "Look at you, all skin and bones. What if death comes to take me in the dead of winter, during the deep freeze? Where will you get the strength to dig up the frozen soil? This way, you'll pour yourself a nice bowl of hot bean soup, top it with some pork rinds, chase it down with a shot of cornelian cherry vodka . . . You'll enjoy it, and I will enjoy it too—it will be like I treated you to a meal!" Tsatur took the money, but when spring came, he showed up at Metaksia's doorstep and dug up her garden.

"What, can't bear to be separated from your shovel?" she joked.

"Yes, I've grown attached to it." Tsatur gave her a lopsided smirk and leaned into the handle of the shovel with his shoulder.

4

He has been coming over for years now. In the spring, he digs up the garden; in the autumn, he helps her pick potatoes and corn. At first, Metaksia kept trying to talk him out of it, but eventually she gave up. If he insists on coming back, he must need to be doing it, she figures. To show her gratitude, she knits winter hats with huge pompoms for Tsatur's kids. He has three little ones, one younger than the next. In those brightly colored hats, they look like cheerful little gnomes.

The silence that hangs over the cemetery is so thick that not even the thrush's trilling song can break it. Metaksia tidies up the grave with great care: she washes the fence and wipes it dry, pulls out the weeds, waters the flowers. As she cleans the accumulated dust and water stains off the gravestone, the years of birth and death etched on it emerge in silent reproach. She holds her breath for longer than she has the strength to. Is it ever possible to reconcile with the young ones dying? Seventeen years of age, an entire lifetime still waiting to be lived.

When she finishes tidying up, she measures frankincense into the memorial lamp and gently strikes a match. While the morning breeze scatters the slightly sweet-smelling, dense smoke, Metaksia sits on a low bench and looks off beyond the horizon, her hands folded in her lap. There, far in the distance, beyond the hunchbacked hill, lies her husband's grave. There's no reaching it now; the wind won't even carry her voice there.

Who could have thought that the happiness allotted to her would turn out to be so short-lived! She grew up in a loving home, with two parents and three older brothers. She never dreamed of getting married; she had been unlucky with her appearance—big-nosed, with a lazy eye and a lipless mouth. Having reconciled herself to her solitary lot, she looked after her numerous nieces and nephews, whom she adored more than life itself. But right after turning forty, she surprised even herself by marrying Razmik's father. They crossed the border to live in his hometown, Omarbeyli, a small hamlet with five Armenian families to seventy Azerbaijani ones.

Razmik was thirteen—a challenging, prickly age—and his father had a hard time dealing with him. People in the village felt sorry for the child: Poor orphan, it's not bad enough that he's lost his mother, but his father didn't even wait long before getting married again. Who has ever heard of a step-mother loving her stepson? She'll have her own kids and start trying to get rid of this one as soon as possible. Metaksia didn't really pay much heed to what people said, but deep down she also feared that having her own child might push Razmik away. That's why she never had the resolve to get pregnant. Four years later, she lost her husband. He died in the middle of the night from a heart attack; he shrieked in pain, arched his back, accidentally hitting her with his elbow, and fell silent.

No matter how much Metaksia implored him, Razmik wouldn't hear of moving to Armenia. "I'm not going anywhere. I have school—I'm graduating this year!" he protested. She gave in but made him promise that they would move to Armenia for him to attend college. Razmik finally caved, on the condition that she would move his parents' ashes to Berd. His request offended her in earnest: "How could you even think that I'd abandon them!" He put his arms around her and broke into tears. From that day on, he took to calling her "Second Mom," or Second for short. She jokingly started calling him First. And so they lived, counting off—First-Second, Second-First.

When the war came, people in villages along the border didn't worry too much about it—all the families had been friends for decades and regularly visited each other. The war was somewhere out there, in the distance, and they were convinced that it wouldn't touch them. God willing, Metaksia rejoined with the rest. That was why she didn't worry when she went to visit her mother, who had taken ill, on the other side of the border. All she did was cook extra food and ask the neighbor to take the laundry off the line when it had dried because Razmik would never have remembered to. Late at night, word reached her that things were restive in Omarbeyli—sounds of gunfire reached the village from the border, and some houses were on fire.

It took Metaksia two full days to make it back. The house stood intact and unharmed; only the gates were bent, as if from a heavy impact. Metaksia ran her fingers over the dent, feeling the roughness of mangled steel in bewilderment. The sheets, stiff from baking in the sun, hung from the laundry lines. It was so quiet inside the house that she could hear the beating of her own heart. Razmik wasn't inside. She eventually found him in the backyard, covered with some dirt and gardening tools that were haphazardly tossed over his body. Metaksia wiped the soil from his face and gathered it into her palms. Without pausing to think about what she was doing, she ate a handful of it, choking in horror and pain, and then poured the rest of it inside her blouse. She lit the stove and warmed up some water. From the cellar, she dragged up the huge basin that she normally used for soaking wool. She carefully laid Razmik inside it. She washed him gently, with bated breath, as if afraid to wake him up. Having realized that she had never once seen him naked before, she started whispering, to overcome her sudden feeling of embarrassment: "You are so well built, my boy, look at that beautiful body of yours. How handsome every part of you is, built for life, for joy, for happiness. If not for this wound in your belly . . . But I'll tie that up so that it doesn't ruin your beauty. I'll dress you in the suit we got for your graduation. I'll brush your unruly hair back—you never let me touch it, you just twisted your head and made annoyed faces, let me go, you said, it's fine as it is! You have such a big, bright forehead, and you wanted to keep it covered . . ."

She had to give up on the idea of putting on his shoes because she couldn't squeeze them on over his crushed feet. "Even killing can be done without inflicting unnecessary pain. Why the torture?" whispered Metaksia, as she wrapped Razmik's feet with towels. Then she dragged a cart out of the shed, lined it with a soft blanket, carefully placed Razmik in it, and rolled him out of their yard. The neighboring homes saw her off in hollow silence. Metaksia never even deigned to give them a parting glance. You say goodbye when you have something to say. She had nothing to say to them.

A GUST OF WIND carried the sharp smell of pines and the distant voice of the awakening river. The sun painted the entire sky gold the moment it peeked from behind Maiden's Cliff. Metaksia rose with a sigh, closed the lamp, and put it back into its special nook. She laid a slice of homemade bread at the head of the gravestone for the heavenly angels. She said goodbye, asked him not to worry and not to miss her too much, promising—Razmik-jan, I'll be back again next week. She left, having carefully shut the wicket gate behind her.

Berd was rising with the laughter of the children, with the coughing of the men, with the hushed voices of the women. Metaksia was walking down the slope, taking in the morning's breath. She had to hurry—the liturgy for the dead was about to begin. Needless to say, the dead have no use for it. The living, though, really need it.

Tights

In February, Mayinants Tsatur turned exactly as old as his father had been when he left for war. Tsatur still remembered how his mother, her arms wrapped around his father's neck, shook her head and begged him, in a voice gone hoarse from crying, "Please don't leave, I won't let you go!" Her bare feet dangled in the air. She was short of stature, with her head barely reaching her husband's shoulder, thin, almost translucent, light as a feather. For her delicate beauty, Arusiak had earned the nickname Doll. Everyone marveled at how a simple village woman could possess so much grace. She toiled in the fields and washed her linens in the river, but nonetheless resembled a porcelain figurine: delicate, slender, outlandish. Tsatur was all of fourteen then, and he stood, pressing his weeping sisters to himself and summoning all of his strength to not break into tears himself. His father caught his eyes and mouthed to him: "Take her away." Tsatur gently took hold of his mother by her armpits and pulled her toward him. He expected her to resist, but she loosened her grip and went limp on his chest.

"Look after the girls," his father said curtly, and walked out without waiting for him to respond. That's how Tsatur remembered him: standing in the doorway, stooping a little—even though he knew that his head did not reach the top of the doorframe, he still bent it slightly when he walked out the door. It was as if he shrank a little every time he left home.

Tsatur couldn't recognize his father in old photos: a large, prematurely gray-haired and incongruously happy man with sloping shoulders and eyes narrowed into tiny slits by laughter. The premature grayness turned out to be hereditary—Tsatur started going gray when he was still in high school and didn't have a single dark hair remaining in his mane by the time he turned thirty. His mother insisted that he looked just like his father; he didn't see the resemblance but didn't argue with her. Not that the resemblance brought her much comfort, but at least it made it easier for her to come to terms with her loss.

In late February, Tsatur turned thirty-three. His sisters came to visit, with their husbands and kids. Everyone stayed up late, reminiscing about childhood. Nobody brought up their father: they all preferred to think about him in private. The guests stayed until close to midnight. The kids were all nodding off by the warm wood-burning stove—bellies full, sleepy, having played their hearts out. While the sisters were saying their goodbyes, Tsatur's wife, Agnessa, handed out small presents: homemade necklaces for the girls, handmade *gulpa*[1] for the boys. The kids all kissed her hands, and only the youngest girl grabbed on to her and pulled her down toward her; her brother chastened her—Have you forgotten that it's hard for her? Tsatur picked up the little girl and brought her face to his wife's. She laughed and kissed the little girl on the nose. Their own children stood in a row, one younger than the next: a boy of five, another boy of four, and a two-and-a-half-year-old girl. Agnessa had always wanted a girl and finally got her wish.

---

1 Hand-knit woolen socks.

They went to bed long after midnight: first they put the kids to sleep, then she did the dishes while he mopped the floors; she wouldn't have managed—it was hard for her to bend down, and she was exhausted after spending the entire day on her feet. "On her feet," Tsatur thought bitterly.

Agnessa, sensing his mood, asked, without turning away from the sink, "What are you thinking about?"

"About how hard things have gotten for you. Mom used to help, but now . . ." He stopped mid-sentence. She shrugged—this is not hard! He nodded in agreement. True, this is not hard.

Tsatur has been burying the people of Berd for seventeen years, ever since the day his father's remains were returned to them. That's when he went to the cemetery and asked Mehrab, the gravedigger, to teach him how to dig a proper grave. Mehrab explained all the intricacies concerning the depth and width of a grave, the properties of the soil and the groundwater. He explained where the head should be and drew a rectangle on the ground with the blade of his shovel. Tsatur handled the rest with his own two hands. While his mother and sisters were at home mourning his father, Tsatur readied his grave. After the funeral, he stayed to work at the cemetery, first as an apprentice to Mehrab, then, after his death, as the gravedigger. And so he lived, ferrying people between this world and the next. He selflessly dedicated himself to raising his sisters, making sure that first the older and then the younger finished school and got married. His mother fretted that he never got married, but he always dismissed her concerns: "Later, later. What talk can there be of marriage now, with so much grief around us?"

One time, he was asked to dig two child-sized graves. At the funeral, only one of the caskets was open. He assumed that the second child must have been maimed beyond recognition by an explosion, but somebody told him that the second casket contained a woman's legs. The family had been sheltering from a bombing in a cellar. It was cold out, and they didn't have time to get properly dressed—they had rushed out of the house in nothing but their sleepwear. The mother fretted that the girl might catch a cold and kept berating herself—if only I had grabbed warm tights for her, if only I had grabbed some tights. During a lull between explosions, she darted out to grab warm clothes, and her daughter chased after her. The child was killed by an explosion, and the mother had both of her legs blown off.

"She's alive, then?" asked Tsatur.

"You call that living?" came the retort.

He first saw Agnessa a few months later. She was sitting on the veranda of her father's house sorting peas. Her hair was cut short and tucked behind her ears, revealing a tiny pink scar on her left cheek, just below the cheekbone. Rumor had it that the scar was the handiwork of her former husband who never forgave her for the death of their child. Tsatur was stunned by the deathly pallor of her fingers and by how, even when she was finished with her task, she kept moving them, as if sorting the air. He watched her, unnoticed, for a while and then couldn't help asking, "Why do you keep moving your fingers?"

"It distracts me from my thoughts," she answered artlessly.

Her mother brought out steaming coffee in a *jezve*;[2] she didn't drink it herself but offered to read the grounds. The coffee patterns on the sides of the cup weren't promising: they portended disappointment, gossip, and worries. "I know what those worries are," said her mother plaintively, setting her cup aside, "I can't find prosthetic legs for her. I've been to

---

2 A small pot with a long handle used for making coffee in Turkey, Armenia, and the Balkans.

12

town three times already, but no luck. She needs to learn to walk again!" She sighed and added bitterly, "My poor child." Agnessa leaned in and pressed her face to her mother's cheek. She didn't kiss her but just sat like that, her lips pressed against her mother's face, and there was so much tenderness and guilelessness in that gesture that Tsatur's heart felt a pinch.

"I'm going to town tomorrow anyway. Why don't you give me the clinic's address?" he said with a cough. And, in order to dispel any doubts, he added, hurriedly, "I have to go for work. I've got to buy a couple of tools."

He used the same pretext to explain his sudden trip to his own mother. Arusiak asked no questions, she just sighed.

Prosthetics were in high demand during the war, so civilian orders were constantly delayed. Nevertheless, Tsatur, after raising a considerable row at the clinic, managed to procure them. He ended up buying two bus tickets for his return trip; the prosthetic legs turned out to be so bulky that he couldn't just carry them in his arms, and he was afraid to put them in the luggage compartment—what if they got damaged? He traveled the entire way back with his arm over them in the seat next to his to keep them from sliding off.

Together, they learned how to do everything anew: how to walk, how to smile, how to breathe. Tsatur proposed with the arrival of spring. She asked him for some time to consider and accepted his proposal reluctantly, after much hesitation. There was no wedding—what revelry could there be amid so much grief? Agnessa dreamed of having a girl, but they had two boys back to back. The doctors, worried about her fragile health, recommended that she wait before having a third, but she didn't heed their advice and finally had a girl. She named her after her dead daughter because she firmly believed that if the name lived on, so did its bearer. Tsatur didn't try to talk his wife out of it even though he wasn't particularly thrilled with the idea of having his daughter named after a dead child. He never mentioned it—what was the point of discussing things that couldn't be changed? Agnessa loved her children more than life itself and always gave them everything they wanted. She fussed over them; she feared, to the point of panic, that they might catch a cold, and so, not sparing any expenses, bought them piles of winter clothes, to make sure they had spares and things to grow into: sweaters, jackets, warm boots, mittens, and scarves. The only thing she never bought were tights. So in the winter her kids waddled around like clumsy goslings, each wearing two pairs of woolen pants. And the funny hats with pompoms made for them by Ginamants Metaksia.

Bundle

God granted Poghosants Vasak two quiet daughters: Arusiak and Anichka. In comparison to the rowdy houses in their neighborhood, his looked orphaned and uninhabited: nobody scaled fences, nobody raced bikes, nobody jumped off the roof into the haystack, screaming as if possessed, nobody carried around pocketfuls of tadpoles. This made Vasak sad, but he didn't grumble. This was what fate had in store for him and Vera—having girls. Still, once in a while, as he observed his neighbors' sons raising a ruckus all over the village, he couldn't help sighing, "A man needs an heir, someone to continue his line!"

A neighbor once tried to offer him some comfort—don't worry, your sons-in-law will be like real sons to you.

"What do you mean, sons-in-law?" asked Vasak, genuinely startled.

"Well, are you planning to marry your girls off? Or will you keep them tucked under your wing forever?" guffawed the neighbor.

Vasak was mortified. He even made a crude joke to mask his embarrassment: "Of course I am," he said, "I'm not going to pickle them." The neighbor had long forgotten about that conversation, but Vasak still called himself an ass every time he recalled it. How could he have said such a thing about his own daughters—I'm not going to pickle them! One word for you—ass!

His daughters were the apples of his eye. The elder, Arusiak, took after her mother—she was delicate, graceful, and thin-boned, a *peri*[1] straight out of a fairy tale. The younger, Anichka, was the spitting image of her father—tall and stately, of sturdy village cast, with broad shoulders, full arms, and a proud posture. Despite the differences in their appearance, the girls had similar personalities and manners. They even insisted on wearing identical clothes, which drove their mother to distraction. How was she supposed to procure two similar coats in different sizes in the backwaters of Murut?[2] Or two pairs of shoes? Vera was good at sewing and knitting, so the girls never had any shortage of dresses and sweaters, but finding outerwear and shoes was always a problem. Since the girls stubbornly refused to wear anything but matching outfits, the parents had to go to town for shopping. While the girls, having enjoyed a frosty milkshake in a tall glass, roamed the spacious halls of a noisy department store, their mother and father languished in endless lines. Having purchased the necessary items with great effort, they would return to their village, vowing never to give in to their daughters' whims again. But exactly a year later, they would have the same discussion and head back to town to shop. They lived for their daughters and did everything to make the girls happy.

Despite being indulged by their parents, Arusiak and Anichka grew up to be modest and hardworking young ladies. They both married in the same year: in January, Arusiak was

---

1 A *peri* (derived from Persian) is a fairy in Armenian fairy tales, usually endowed with unearthly beauty as well as magical abilities.

2 Currently Üçbulaq, until 1999 known as Murut, a village in Azerbaijan.

given away to a husband in remote Berd, and Anichka was betrothed in December. Unlike her sister, she found a suitor in Murut, a fact that was a source of boundless joy to her parents, who were happy that at least one of their girls would remain by their side.

Vasak had a brief but frank talk with each son-in-law. He picked a good time to pull them aside and told them, in chilling detail, exactly *what* he would do to them if they hurt his daughters. Mercifully, both sons-in-law were blessed with a good sense of humor and didn't take offense; instead, with a hearty laugh, they promised to duly note their father-in-law's words. They turned out to be excellent husbands, and with time, just as the neighbor had predicted, came to be like sons for Vasak.

Vera had long complained about her legs—first of dull pain and feeling pins and needles, and then of losing all feeling in them. Vasak kept trying to convince her to consult a specialist, but she waved him off, saying that it would eventually just go away. She took to bed right after Anichka's wedding. Multiple trips to clinics and hospitals did nothing to improve her condition, and by sixty, she completely lost mobility in her legs. Still, she had no intention of giving up on life; she mastered using the wheelchair and went back to handling all the laundry and cooking. Anichka checked in on her parents daily and helped out with cleaning, gardening, and milking the cow. Arusiak visited once a month and stayed for a few days. Life, even if not very easy, went on its course, counting out months and then years, and its monotony brought comfort to Vera and Vasak. "Thank you, Lord, for the opportunity to exist and to be happy," she would say. "Thank you," Vasak echoed. They slowly grew old, surrounded by the love of their daughters and their husbands, and later of the grandchildren who finally turned the once-quiet house into a raucous gathering place: they tirelessly scaled fences, jumped off the roof into the haystack screaming as if possessed, packed tadpoles into their pockets, and raced their bikes. Anichka had three sons, Arusiak had one son and two daughters. Vasak adored all of his grandkids but had a special place in his heart for Arusiak's son Tsatur. There was something special about his eldest grandson that filled the old man's heart with boundless love. "You are this world's conscience," he liked to say, caressing his grandson's unruly hair. Tsatur would smile back, embarrassed, too shy to contradict his grandfather.

YEARS LATER, WHEN THE PAIN hadn't really subsided but at least shrunk enough to make breathing possible again, Arusiak often asked herself what she would have done differently had she known everything in advance. Would she have stayed in Murut to share her family's terrible fate, or would she have begged them to relocate to Berd? But she would never have been able to persuade her father; he always said, "My place is where my ancestors are buried."

"I should have stayed," Arusiak wept then, "people belong where their roots are."

The war escalated seemingly overnight; one day, it was still possible to call Murut, but by the next day the connection was cut, and no word about their loved ones got through. Arusiak was beside herself; she cried day and night and refused to get out of bed. The kids did what they could to keep the household running. Her husband went to the border every day to meet the refugees. People were pouring in, exhausted, lost. Some, who never got used to the reality of what had happened, lost their minds along the way; others descended into madness after they had made it to safety. Her husband kept searching for his wife's relatives because he knew that they had nowhere else to go but Berd.

One day, an old woman caught his eye. After she had crossed the border, she did not follow the others but lowered herself onto a rock by the roadside. Having eased herself into a seated position, she kicked off her shoes, pulled down the bottom of her skirt to cover her swollen and bleeding feet, and set down a small, soiled bundle. His breath caught in his throat—he recognized the scarf that Arusiak had made for her sister as a present: red poppies against a blue background. She had embroidered them with her own hands, weaving silver thread into the edges of the flower petals. He approached the old woman to find out where she had gotten that scarf. She lifted her eyes, and he almost choked in horror—it was Anichka.

In a dull monotone, she told him that she was at her parents' house when disaster struck. Her mother was sitting on the veranda, her father was chopping wood, and she was tidying up in the attic. First she heard screaming, then she saw through the attic window how her father was axed to death and how her mother, who had long been wheelchair-bound, rose up and, calling to her husband, stumbled down the stairs, how they reached her, hit her over the head with the back of the axe and dragged her toward the fence by her hair—you remember, don't you, mom's braids, still beautiful in her old age? She was dragged by those beautiful gray braids, leaving behind a dark, wet trail, and it wouldn't dry up, it wouldn't dry up.

Anichka gave him a small, guilty smile and added, "I don't remember anything that happened after that." She fell silent. She tried to shove her feet back into her shoes, but they were too swollen. She set them aside, pressed the bundle to her chest, and got up with considerable effort.

"Take me away from here. Please."

He took the bundle from her, untied it, and looked inside. His face changed.

"PLEASE DON'T LEAVE, I won't let you go!" Arusiak begged him the next morning. His son stood in the corner, pressing his weeping sisters to himself and summoning all of his strength to not break into tears himself. His father caught his eyes and mouthed to him: "Take her away." Tsatur gently took hold of his mother by her armpits and pulled her toward him. He expected her to resist, but she loosened her grip and went limp on his chest.

"Look after the girls," his father said curtly, and walked out before Tsatur could answer. That's how Tsatur remembered him: in the doorway, slightly stooping—even though he knew that his head did not reach the top of the doorframe, he still bent it slightly when he walked out the door. It was as if he shrank a little every time he left home.

Baghardj

Zarginants Atanes wakes up at the crack of dawn. The first thing he does is lean awkwardly over the edge of the bed to turn off his alarm clock so its unceremonious and annoying chiming does not wake up his sleeping son. Then he opens the window, climbs back under his blanket, and lies with his eyes closed, taking in the sounds of Berd as it stirs itself awake: the distant, barely audible whisper of the river, the singing of the birds, the indignant gobbling of the perennially discontented turkeys, the honking of the combative geese. The garbage truck passes through, its ancient motor hissing. Atanes is convinced that the truck is as old as the world. Seasons, generations, and centuries come and go; the only thing that doesn't change is the metallic pile of junk that, desperately fuming and choking on its own smoke, continues to cart endless, useless garbage out of Berd with the determination of an ant.

The neighbor's rooster, perched on top of the fence, is crowing its heart out. Atanes smiles as he remembers a recent episode: The rooster roamed the veranda, his claws clicking against the floorboards and his yellow eyes covetously trained on the trays of freshly roasted wheat laid out to cool. It wasn't that the rooster pecked at it—he was no fool to burn himself on scalding grains, but he looked disgruntled and even menacing. The sight of him sent Levon into peals of gurgling, quiet laughter: "Dad, look, Dad, Peto!"

To Levon, all roosters are Peto.

All dogs—Sevo.

All horses—Chalo.[1]

All people—Person. That's exactly what he says: Person came, Person left. Only about one woman he says: Gentle Person came. Pretty, he adds.

Everyone is entitled to his own idea of beauty, and even then, it evolves considerably over the course of one's lifetime. But for Levon, it is as constant as it is certain—a pretty person is whoever brings him a sweet treat. That's why Poghosants Anichka is a Pretty Person. After all, she often brings him *baghardj*,[2] which she makes with thick cream instead of water, flouting the traditional recipe, and layers it with roasted almonds.

"Dad, Dad, look, Gentle Person coming. Pretty!" rejoices Levon, spotting Anichka as she opens the gate.

"Levon-jan? It's past noon, and you're still in bed?" Anichka chides him with feigned sternness as she climbs the stairs leading to the veranda. The stairs require considerable effort on her part; she groans and leans her palms into her knees with every step. At first, Atanes would try to help her, but he eventually gave it up because she angrily rebuffed him, insisting that she'd manage on her own for as long as her legs carried her.

---

1 Peto, Sevo, and Chalo are common names given to roosters, dogs, and horses, respectively. Peto derives from the Russian word for rooster, *petukh*; Sevo, literally, a blackie, from the Armenian word for black, *sev*; Chalo, from the Armenian word *chal*, multicolored.

2 A flat, pie-shaped dessert with ornately decorated edges, a staple of Armenian cuisine.

Baghardj

Levon is propped up on a daybed, the bottom part of his body tightly swaddled. He reaches for Anichka with his thin, long arms, the only part of his body that's not wrapped up. Gentle Person coming. Pretty.

Anichka sits down next to him and unwraps the bundle, revealing golden pieces of sweet *baghardj*, and only then is able to catch her breath.

While Levon is enjoying the treat, she and Atanes leisurely chat. About how the roof needs patching. How the fence is leaning and prone to collapse. How the days keep getting shorter and the nights longer, and how that's not because winter is coming but because they are getting older. How they are due for a visit to the cemetery soon because Green Sunday is just around the corner, and the Saturday of Souls comes right after.[3] How you have to prepare for it ahead of time, because you can't show up to pay respects at an untidied grave.

Then Atanes heats up some water, and together they bathe Levon. Full and content, he diligently splashes and rejoices—"Dad, nice, right?"

"Nice, very nice, Levon-jan."

They apply special ointment to the bedsores on his nape, shoulder blades, and lower back. Anichka makes it herself; she heats up vegetable oil, stirs in beeswax, and sets it aside to cool completely.

After Levon falls asleep, they linger on the veranda for a while longer. Atanes makes them tea, while Anichka darns old, worn-out linens. They take their tea in their own ways: she with tiny bites of sugar in her mouth, he with fruit preserves.

---

3 In the Armenian Apostolic Church, Green Sunday is the second Sunday after the resurrection of Jesus Christ. "Saturday of Souls," observed several times a year by all Orthodox Christian churches, is a day reserved for the commemoration of the dead.

"You should have said yes when I asked you to marry me," Atanes breaks the silence. "It would have been easier if we were together."

Anichka looks at him.

"Do you really believe that?"

Atanes doesn't answer.

"See, you don't even believe it yourself, but you keep repeating the same thing," concludes Anichka.

She leaves in the evening, when the timid light of the first stars speckles the sky.

Afterward, Atanes lies awake in his bed for a long time, peering into the indifferent eyes of the night. Levon is asleep next to him, his hands tucked under his cheek, like a child. The war stole everyone else from Atanes; it would have stolen his son as well, but it failed—the force of the explosion tossed Levon out of the bombed bus right before it fell into the gorge. Levon used to be a healthy, sturdy young man; now he is crippled and destined to remain a child forever. He doesn't even know how old he is. And to think that they celebrated his thirty-fifth birthday just last winter!

Anichka had it worse, although who's to say with what yardstick one should measure pain? Her entire family perished in the pogroms, and all she was able to recover were the charred remains of her youngest son. She tied his ashes into a bundle, carried them over the border, and buried them. When she heard about Levon, she came to visit him with *baghardj*, which had been her children's favorite treat. She has been coming to visit for years. At first Atanes kept trying to turn down the treat because he didn't want to grow dependent on anyone, but eventually he grew used to her visits and even looked forward to them. Once, he even worked up the courage to propose marriage to her. To this, she responded that between the two of them, they would have too much grief to carry. "On our own, at least we can manage somehow," she said.

Atanes falls asleep long after midnight and wakes up at the crack of dawn. The first thing he does is lean awkwardly over the edge of the bed to turn off his alarm clock so that its unceremonious and persistent chiming does not wake up his sleeping son. Then he opens the window, climbs back under his blanket and lies with his eyes closed, taking in the sounds of Berd as it stirs itself awake. He spends his morning over routine household chores: cleaning, weeding and watering the garden, washing and cooking. After the midday meal, he carries Levon out onto the veranda, props him up on the daybed, and sits down next to him. And together they settle to wait until Anichka will come over, bringing with her the golden pieces of the blessed *baghardj*. Levon always eats it as if he is tasting sunlight.

Loneliness

Muradants Andro knows something about predawn Berd unknown even to the birds that herald the arrival of the new day with their ebullient song. While their idle chirping, rising on the edge of the valley, drifts, before gaining momentum and soaring up to the top of the hill that greets the sun with a deep bow, Andro's rusty, ramshackle truck, ancient like the world itself, spitting heavy petroleum fumes and burned machine oil along the way, huffing and periodically driving one of its wheels into a ditch that has been washed out by endless rains and hardened by the baking sun, goes yard to yard and collects transient human garbage that rustles like onion peels.

"Can't you at least fix your muffler? This monstrosity wakes us up with its roaring before our alarm clocks!" grumble the inhabitants of Berd.

Without shutting off the engine, Andro pulls on the hand brake with a metallic screech, climbs out of the cabin, loudly banging the door, and methodically dumps the contents of the trash containers into the back of the truck, never failing to give the bottom of each bin a good pounding with his fist to allow the clumps of paper, potato peels, and eggshells one last chance to unstick from the wet walls, before meticulously arranging the bins in a neat row along the side of the road.

"This jalopy was built before mufflers were invented. Why shouldn't it roar?" he eventually deigns to respond. And then, after a small pause, he adds good-naturedly, "What's your problem? It's morning already, time to wake up anyway."

"What do you mean, time to wake up? My alarm's not set to go off for another hour!"

"God smiles upon those who rise early."

By the time the thousand-voices-strong bird chorus unites in a powerful laudatory song and reaches the Eastern Hill, rousing it from its ancient slumber, Muradants Andro has finished his regular morning route and steered his truck toward the reservoir, behind which, if you keep driving for another thirty minutes, lies a sprawling landfill. He knows this road by heart and could make the drive with his eyes closed. On the right hand stretches a cypress grove, propping up the sky with its sharp-tipped cupolas. Further down, a river snakes through thickets of reeds, its silvery scales glittering in the sun. The frogs are quiet, hiding silently under rocks, and their croaking won't be heard again until evening, but an oriole is singing as only an oriole can, in a tender, soul-soothing voice. On the opposite bank of the river, tobacco fields are growing green, and Andro wrinkles his nose as he recalls the scratchy smell of the caustic juice permanently eaten into his mom's and aunts' hands. While he and his cousins ran around with improvised bows and arrows slung over their shoulders, playing cowboys and Indians ("A-andro! Hey, Andro, play whatever you want, but stay where I can see you!" his mother would shout at the top of her lungs when she lost sight of him), the women would position themselves on wooden benches, wrap their faces in scarves, leaving only a narrow slit for their eyes, and string tobacco leaves using long steel needles. Now, if he tuned out all external noise, he could still hear the constant, monotonous movement of their deft fingers, dyed black from the tobacco juice. The women would pierce the stem at the base with the needle and gently, so as not to tear the leaf itself, ease it onto the string while carefully monitoring the spacing of the leaves—the smaller ones could go right next to each other, but the bigger ones needed more room, otherwise they would trap moisture and rot before ever having a chance to dry. The strings of leaves would be hung, shielded by a canopy, not too low so that the sun and the wind both had a chance to frolic between them unimpeded, drying them gently and softly. The work was demanding and labor-intensive; by the end of each day, his mother's hands stung so badly that she couldn't contain her groaning. She rubbed them with apple vinegar and rendered duck fat before bed, but it didn't bring her much relief. "It feels like my fingers are setted on fire!" she complained. "Set!" he'd correct her with an eye roll. "Set," his mother would agree, but then invariably go on to make the same mistake the next day.

THE COFFIN MADE HER look small. Her feet didn't even reach the bottom. She looked like she wasn't dead but simply dozing and could be startled awake if you called her. Andro couldn't get enough of looking at her: she was beautiful in that stern, primal way typical of people who live in the mountains—tall, lean, with irregular but attractive facial features. Her hands, which had been hardened by decades of manual labor and which had known no rest when she was alive, now lay on her chest like dead weight. Wrapped in dark wool cloth, they looked like two pieces of stone that pressed her down to the ground for eternity. Andro studiously avoided looking at them because otherwise he would break into tears. "A-andro! Hey, Andro, play whatever you want, but stay where I can see you!" she would shout at the top of her lungs, squinting myopically as she strained to identify her child in the boisterous crowd. "Mom, why do you have to yell like that!" he would snap at her every time. "I'm afraid you may not hear me," she'd explain with a guilty smile.

Andro was certain that she had called out to him. She had gotten trapped underneath the heavy, smoke-soaked beams, underneath pieces of brittle old roof tiles and chunks of the exploded chimney, underneath bundles of dried apples and prunes, ears of corn, rectangles of honeycomb that had burst open, sending the golden-amber, sticky, sour-sweet mountain honey over her gray hair, down her back and her legs, which were wedged under the hodgepodge of useless items she had hoarded and never brought herself to discard because each of them was a keepsake, even the old, completely rusted cart wheel that could have been tossed and forgotten about, and yet she insisted on keeping it, just as she insisted on keeping the worm-eaten chest riveted along the edges with brass plates because her grandfather, the welder, had embossed them with his own hands, beating out with a steel punch and a narrow mallet an uncomplicated but still fairly ornamental pattern; nor could she ever part with the cracked ginger-colored clay pots, a keepsake from her other grandfather, a potter, or with old carpets, riddled with holes and worn to rags, or with wicker baskets whose sides bristled with broken twigs, because her grandmother's hands had once touched them. All of that junk—useless and senseless, yet dear to his mother's heart—had collapsed at once, taking down with it whatever had managed to withstand the explosion, and forming an airtight, solid sarcophagus around her. She had curled up into a ball, and no flying pieces had hit her; she must have lain there in a fetal pose, her knees pressed to her stomach and her arms folded on her chest, helpless and unable to move, calling out to her son. And he had failed to hear her.

It was an old brick house, with a worn tiled roof and rickety shutters, with squeaky, loose floorboards and walls hunched over by time. Back in his day, Andro's great-grandfather had gotten his allotment in a remote area about a day-and-a-half's travel away, so at first he wanted to just abandon it. But the soil there proved to be so fertile that after long deliberations, he decided to build a small, sturdy dwelling on it after all. Andro's mother spent her weekends there as long as the weather held up, and toward the end of October, when the tobacco had been picked and processed, she always stayed there for a week or two, readying the beehives for the winter, picking the last, already frost-kissed raspberries, making tangy jam from the dusty-looking blackthorn berries, and tilling her garden before winter. Andro would come to pick her up on a prearranged day, and they would move all the winter preserves she had prepared back to their house. Sometimes he offered to stay with her, but she always refused; she wanted some alone time, a break from other people.

The last October of her life coincided with the start of yet another twist in the war. With Berd being unrelentingly shelled for an entire week, Andro couldn't help but feel relief that his mom was safe in the remote house. He wasn't concerned for her safety, because nobody would ever waste bombs on unpopulated areas—it only makes sense to drop bombs in places where the harvest of potential victims will be bountiful.

When, upon his arrival, he discovered a rubble-filled crater in place of the house, he didn't believe his eyes; he stood looking around for a few minutes, thinking that he might have

30

taken a wrong turn. Then, coming to his senses, he rushed to dig the wreckage with his bare hands. It was nearly dawn when he found his mother. He wept as he freed her from the stone dust, bunches of dried mint, torn pieces of old newspapers, honey, and broken roof tiles. He eased her out gently, as if extracting a pearl from an oyster shell.

He talked to her the entire drive back. He asked her how he was supposed to go on living with the unbearable burden of being orphaned. How he was supposed to mourn her without letting other people see his tears. How he was supposed to forgive himself for the fact that not a single string stirred in his soul while she lay there calling out to him, for not being there with her. His mother lay curled up on the back seat; he had tried to straighten her arms at least, but her stiffened body refused to obey, and she rested with her knees pressed to her chest, as if simply asleep. Beautiful, young, untouched by rot.

Andro stopped by the reservoir and sat in the car, crying and wailing. Driven by unbearable anguish, he got out, leaving the door wide open; for some reason, he was afraid to slam it shut lest he disturb his mother's repose. He stood on the very edge of the water, absorbing the muteness of the sky—an incorruptible silence that extinguished any hope of salvation. The silence was deafening, the clouds were low to the ground, the air was still, taut, suffocating—like a warm, overstuffed feather blanket. Andro knew for certain that from that moment onward, nothing would frighten him more than this stony, dejected silence. "God, how can you be this indifferent and deaf to human suffering?" he shouted. That shout—drawn out, full of rage, throat-lacerating—emanated from his chest in unbearable despair and hovered over the black water for a long time, disturbing its ripples. He didn't so much hear his mother's voice as feel it. Emerging out of nowhere, the voice didn't speak; instead, it filled Andro's pain-shattered heart. "I hear you," it rustled and died out, leaving behind a feeling of irreparable loss and dull grief.

MURADANTS ANDRO KNOWS about predawn Berd what even the birds that herald the arrival of a new day with their cheerful song don't. While their idle chirping, rising from the edge of the valley, soars up to the summit of the ancient Eastern Hill, awakening it from its stony slumber, Andro's rusty, ramshackle truck, coughing out heavy petroleum fumes and burned machine oil, huffing and periodically driving one of its wheels into the crusted-over ditch, goes yard to yard, scaring off animals and waking people at an ungodly hour.

People of Berd feel exasperated, but they put up with it. They know that for Andro, silence is torture. After all, our conscience speaks to us in the voices of the departed. Just tune out the external noise, and you will hear them.

To Live

———

Akunants Karapet was killed on the stoop of his own house. When the neighbors rushed over, they found him slumped against the doorframe, his hands in his lap and his gaze fixed on the corner of the house where the projectile had exploded. The dog was quietly whimpering in the doghouse, afraid to show its nose. The chickens dashed back and forth along the picket fence, clucking frantically, but the sight of people calmed them down. Only one of them continued its mindless sprint, cackling hoarsely.

"Go catch it and twist its neck," Maro instructed her eldest grandson.

He obeyed without a word. Having tossed the killed chicken into the outhouse, he rinsed his hands off in the barrel of rainwater—the water had stagnated and reeked of dampness and wet moss. He squeamishly sniffed at his fingertips, wiped them off on his pants, and rushed back inside. By then, his younger brothers and grandmother had already laid Karapet's body out on a daybed.

The second projectile exploded so close that it felt as if their house had been hit. The walls squeaked and quaked, the cupboard came crashing down in the kitchen, and the plastic

that had long replaced the glass in the window frames burst
into small pieces from the force of the explosion.

"To the cellar!" shouted Maro and grabbed Karapet's body
by the shoulders. The boys resolutely moved her aside—we'll
handle this. Lifting Karapet didn't pose much of a challenge;
in his old age, he had grown gaunt, and his neck protruded
from his shirt like the dried-up stem of an overripe pear.
Maro's eldest grandson frowned, somewhat inappropriately
recalling the crunching sound that the chicken's neck had
made. They didn't have far to go, just down the stairs and about
ten steps to the right, but they had to hurry so as not to get
caught in the next round of shelling. Maro limped behind her
grandchildren, mumbling curses under her breath: "May you
turn into stone, you shameless tribe! May your dead ones come
out of their graves to take you with them to the other world!
Who has ever seen such a thing, bombing peaceful homes?"

The third projectile exploded just as the eldest grandson
slammed the door behind their dog—it rushed into the
cellar, whimpering piteously, tripped over the high step, lost its
balance, fell, slamming its big-eared head into the flour chest,
and squealed in pain. The speckled hens, out of their minds with
fright, darted around the yard, struggling to breathe through
their hoarse clucking. The next explosion hit even closer, as if
right next to them, instantly putting an end to the chickens'
frightened squawks. Maro was knocked to the floor, along with
her grandkids. The eldest, in one long, gravity-defying leap,
reached the youngest and covered him with his body, but the
youngest immediately wriggled free: "You take care of yourself."
Then he started to get up and go upstairs to check what was
going on in the yard, but his brothers didn't let him: "Where
on earth do you think you're going?" The youngest shoved them
with his elbows, for which he immediately got a smack upside

the head. Maro shushed them, nodding in the direction of the deceased: "This is not the time!" The grandkids, immediately contrite, simmered down.

Akunants Karapet lay on the earthen floor, one arm thrown sideways, the other awkwardly bent at the elbow and pinned under him. Maro closed his eyelids, marveling at how enormous his pupils were. She folded his arms on his chest, tightly securing his wrists with a handkerchief; since there was no knowing when they would be able to bury him, it was best to do everything properly straight away. Rumor had it that when they were burying Muradants Satik, whose absence had gone unnoticed for an entire week, they ended up having to break her stiffened arms because there was no other way to cross them on her chest. Maro didn't want the same to happen to Karapet. The wound in his temple was tiny, and very little blood trickled out, no more than three tablespoons. "Shame on you, measuring human blood in tablespoons," Maro chided herself. She pulled off her belt and tied up Karapet's feet. She arranged her cardigan over his legs to cover up the wet spot that was spreading over his trousers—she didn't think there was any need for her grandsons to see how his urine was draining out. Then she folded her headscarf in four and tied up his chin. "The worst thing about death isn't its existence so much as the fact that it enjoys deforming and humiliating the human body. It's no better than an ignoble adversary, who, having vanquished his opponent, desecrates his fallen body," thought Maro bitterly.

The dog was whining, its muzzle buried in the cupped hands of the eldest grandchild, who quietly petted the dog on its head. When the next explosion came, he picked up the dog and hugged it to his chest. The dog sighed loudly and emitted a truly human-sounding sob but then immediately stopped. Projectiles were exploding all over Berd. The walls of the old stone houses trembled, the last remaining glass panes burst out of the windows, and the animals went into a frenzy. Human fear—bulky, billowing—breathlessly spread from yard to yard, filling the cracks between the rows of firewood, the slanting chimneys, the attics, and the crawl spaces. Hopelessness and misery reigned supreme; it was as if anything that could inspire hope had been snuffed out at once.

Maro sat leaning against the wall, her eyes fixed on the corner of the cellar where Karapet lay. The two of them had spent their entire lives feuding. He would knock his fence over onto her red currant bushes while mending it, as if by accident; she would "forget" to turn off the hose, and the flowing water would turn his garden into a swamp. Many times it almost came to blows between them: Karapet had a short fuse and was mean-spirited, and quickly became unhinged when provoked. He'd raise his hand, and you'd think he was about to strike. But no, at the last second he would clench his hand into a fist and draw it back.

"Why don't you go ahead and hit me?" Maro would sneer.

Karapet would walk away, shoving her hard with his shoulder.

If you asked her now how their enmity started, she wouldn't be able to tell you. At first, they lived side by side, with their families, and everyone seemed happy. She had a son, he had a son. One day they both woke up alone: Maro's husband had taken Karapet's wife and son and moved to a different village. Berd bubbled over with gossip and then forgot all about it, but Maro and Karapet seemed to have petrified. And so they lived, steeped in their respective misery. In the early days, they dropped in on each other to commiserate, but eventually they stopped. Maro forgave her husband easily; she sent her son and then her grandkids to visit. Karapet never exchanged another word with his wife. He also rarely saw his son; he couldn't let go of the fact that he had left without saying a word, although what can you possible expect from a four-year-old? Eventually Karapet turned against Maro as well. She ignored his hostility initially, but then started snapping back. That's how they quarreled.

Their sons were both thirty when the war broke out. They both went to fight. Both perished, leaving never-healing wounds in their parents' hearts. The day his son died, Karapet came over, but he didn't have the resolve to go inside, so he just stayed on her veranda until the next morning. When she came outside, she found him asleep, his head resting in the crook of his elbow. His entire shirtsleeve was soaked through with tears. She sat next to him and patted him on his shoulder. He started sobbing in his sleep. He made up with his wife at the funeral—"made up" in the sense that they hugged each other and cried before going their own separate ways.

"Tati, hey, Tati, listen!" her grandson's voice calling her snapped Maro out of her reverie.

"What is it?" She looked around and dried her eyes with the back of her hand. The explosions were becoming more and more distant. With any luck, they'd cease altogether any minute, and then it would become possible to come out of hiding, to tally up the living and to bury the dead.

"Tati!" Her youngest grandson was staring at Maro with his father's eyes. That was the reason his brothers and his grandmother let him get away with everything—he was the spitting image of his father, just as dark-eyed and ginger-freckled. "Why couldn't we just leave grandpa Karapet upstairs? He's dead anyway."

"Dead or alive, a human being is a human being," said Maro.

A rooster crowed loudly, echoed by a second and a third one. The birds could always tell the end of a shelling. Maro got up and unlatched the cellar door. It was time to come out—time to go on living.

37

Baklava

Old Maro's daughter-in-law was killed on the third day of the downpour, when the roads were completely washed out and the trees were so soaked that they couldn't support their limply sagging branches and their drooping wet leaves. The heavenly river just flowed and flowed, washing the world with its cool streams.

Maro, overcome with a sense of foreboding, kept trying to talk her daughter-in-law out of leaving, despite the fact that she herself had baked a huge tray of baklava just the night before: paper-thin dough encasing an ethereal layer of whipped egg whites with sugar and walnuts, a golden crust generously soaked in cinnamon-spiced honey warmed up in a water bath; her in-laws liked cinnamon, so she didn't skimp on it. A sixtieth birthday was serious cause for celebration, so Maro's daughter-in-law had decided to surprise her mother who lived on the other side of Owl Mountain. Her brothers arrived two days before her scheduled departure. Three silent giants—when they entered the house, it seemed to immediately run out of air; Maro even kept the windows open all night to make sure the guests could breathe. The brothers were on their way to town with Molokan[1] specialties: macerated apples, pickled cabbage with cranberries, pies stuffed with farmer's cheese and berries. On their way back, they came to pick up their sister. Maro was quick to agree at first, but then started feeling apprehensive. Yet try as she might, she couldn't talk her daughter-in-law out of going.

When she was already walking out, Maro made one last effort to stop her—she planted herself in the doorway, blocking the way, and shook her head: "No, please don't go, my child, I'm begging you, listen to me, stay."

It all happened at the end of the mountain pass, when the car, ducking out of the sheet of rain, found itself on a looping road leading to Owl Gorge. Maro's daughter-in-law was sitting in the back seat, pressed between her two older brothers, the tray with baklava balanced on her knees; her youngest brother was in the front passenger seat, and Krnatants Khoren was at the wheel. He knew where to brake and where to hit the gas while keeping the car as far as possible from the road shoulder.

When they got to the most perilous portion of the road, he gave everyone a heads-up—we're going to speed through here. The brothers leaned in, shielding their sister; the engine revved, gaining momentum. Beyond the pass, rain was pouring down from the sky, and the clouds dragged over the earth and got tangled in the jagged treetops. Khoren counted down—five, four, three, two, one, as he steered the car toward the safety of the gorge.

---

1 A breakaway Russian religious group dating back to the eleventh century, whose name derives from the Russian word for milk, *moloko*, because its adherents used dairy during Russian Orthodox fasting days. Persecuted throughout the history of the Russian Empire, they were resettled in various remote parts of it, including what is now Armenia and Azerbaijan.

Nobody heard the gunshot but everyone saw at once
how, seemingly out of nowhere, a crack materialized on the
windshield; it was expanding in all directions, so quickly that
it seemed to be running away from itself. A tiny circle—the
bullet hole—was barely visible in its center. The youngest
brother looked back and immediately broke into sobs. His
sister, a surprised expression on her face, was smiling,
lopsidedly, with the left corner of her mouth, just like she did
as a child.

Maro was sixty-two years old when her daughter-in-law
died, leaving behind her small children. She was the first
person to die on the road between Berd and Owl Gorge.
Nowadays, such silence reigns there during the day that you
can hear the mountain flowers blooming, but once darkness
falls, the hooting of the owls will keep you up all night. That's
now. Back then, all was silent. Not even the wind sang, because
back then the war ruled over that mountain pass.

Old Maro passed away when her eldest grandchild turned
twenty. She welcomed him home when he finished his military service, took to bed the very next day, and departed on
Easter Eve, quiet and peaceful. She was laid to rest between
her son and her daughter-in-law; the war had taken her son
at the very beginning, and his wife—only a little later. It was
probably destined that way, that he had to go first and that
in a car carrying four grown men, her daughter-in-law had
to be the one to die, and Maro kept telling herself that it was
all part of some divine design beyond human comprehension
as she tried to fight the bitterness that ate away at her soul;
but she never managed to overcome it, for she never again
made baklava—phyllo dough, whipped egg whites with
sugar and walnuts, with a golden crust generously soaked in

cinnamon-spiced honey. The last baklava she ever made was left on her dead daughter-in-law's knees; another one never came to be, for how can there be baklava when the heart just aches and aches?

Gulpa

T he cow had to be slaughtered after all. Khoren was loath to do it and kept delaying it for as long as possible, hoping she would recover. He didn't dare leave her with the herd and instead took her outside the village, to the riverbank, where he himself watched her as she made a visible effort to graze and as she drank, panting through sobs.

"What is it, Malishka?" he awkwardly tried to soothe the cow, petting her golden-yellow crest. He wanted her to live so much it hurt. The cow mooed in agony, shook her head, and stared at him with her extinguished eyes that were lined with eyelashes bleached out by the sun. Khoren would feel her burning nose with his palm and groan sadly. He had already done everything that might have helped her: he rubbed her belly with a wisp made of hay, and he even made her drink infusions of wild mint and thyme. He knew that these curative measures were of no use, but he couldn't sit around and watch his cow's suffering from the sidelines.

He confided the real reason for Malishka's illness only to his mother. She heard him out without saying a word, soundlessly moved her lips, then set aside her knitting, strained her neck, as if scanning for someone in the yard, and asked, with concern, "Is Khoren back from school?"

For a second, Khoren was caught off guard, but then he reassured her—yes, he's back.

"Good," she nodded.

He rose, indecisively shuffled his feet, and wanted to ask her a question, but then decided against it. Instead, he leaned over with a groan and kissed the edge of her warm headdress that smelled of the sun. The soft fringe tickled his face, and he had to bite his lip in order to stop the rising bitter sigh from escaping. Then he asked, without hoping for an answer, "So, I'm gonna head out then, Ma?"

She didn't respond.

Malishka was dying of hurt. Khoren was certain of this, but he couldn't tell this to anyone except his mother. Nobody would have believed him anyway. Who could have known that this could happen to her, of all cows, when she was so cautious and easily spooked. She had been timid since birth and rarely let anyone near her. When she was eventually put out to pasture, she trailed after the shepherd's gampr[1]—she went where he went. She felt safer that way. The dog ignored her at first but eventually grew annoyed and even nipped at her side once, not very hard but enough to hurt her feelings. Malishka mooed pitifully and broke into tears. "Her tears were this big, each practically the size of a grape," said the shepherd to Khoren, closing the tip of his thumb over the second joint of his index finger to indicate the size of the cow's tears, as he relayed the incident that night. Khoren barely contained his urge to kick the gampr in the belly. The dog, sensing Khoren's mood, lowered his muzzle and looked askance, backing away guiltily until he disappeared from view. But Malishka was like

1 An Armenian breed of herding dogs.

a child—she forgave easily and forever, and was back to trailing after the dog the very next day. Fearful of her owner's temper, the gampr put up with the cow's attachment and refrained from snapping at her. Then, to everyone's surprise, he grew attached to her. From that point on, after making a lap around the herd, he would return to where she grazed. He stayed by her side in bad weather because Malishka was afraid of thunder and, upon hearing its first distant roll, invariably tried to hide in the worst possible places: she would duck under an overhang in the cliff, from where a single misstep would have sent her tumbling down into the gorge, or she would run down into the ravine, from which she then had trouble climbing because she slipped on the wet soil.

Once she fell back from the herd and lost her way. Khoren found her by the high-pitched howling of the jackals—he ran in the direction of their soul-numbing howls without looking where he stepped. By the time he got to Malishka, the jackals had surrounded her on all sides and were slowly closing in, yapping and barking. Khoren was amazed by the expression in her eyes—she was staring into the distance over the jackals' heads. She didn't make a single effort to defend herself; she just stood there like a stone statue, like a monument to herself. He forced his way into the thick of the snarling pack and tossed the beasts aside. By the time the gampr found them, Khoren's arms were torn to the flesh, and he had a deep bitemark on his left ankle. Who knows what might have happened to him had it not been for the shepherd dog, whose furious attack forced the jackals back until they reluctantly retreated, communicating with each other in repulsive, plangent yelps. Malishka didn't even acknowledge Khoren's presence; she stumbled off, stepping awkwardly because her full udder made it difficult to walk. He caught up to her, put his arms around her neck, petted her face and her ears. She mooed with hurt and recrimination. He milked her a little for relief and took her down to the river to drink. She didn't drink, but the rustling of the river calmed her down, and she seemed to recover a little, even appearing placated. The way back was long and difficult, and Malishka frequently took breaks, gasped convulsively, shook her head as if shellshocked, and periodically tried to cross to the other side of the road. Khoren patiently coaxed her back, kissed her forehead, and tried to reason with her.

It was very late when they got home. Everyone was asleep except for his oldest granddaughter, Lusine, who was dozing off on the veranda curled up under a home-knit blanket, waiting for their return. She hugged her grandfather, and, without even asking any questions, said everything he could have said: "You were out searching for a long time, you must be tired." Khoren nodded yes, there was no other way, *tsavd tanem*.[2] "I'll deal with her, you go rest," Lusine assured him and led the cow to the barn. When she came back, she helped him clean the wound on his ankle and applied ointment to it. "Jackals?"

"Jackals, damn them all!"

"You should go to the clinic tomorrow."

"I should," agreed Khoren, but he never went, because he didn't get around to it.

Malishka never recovered from that fright. She lost her appetite and quickly started losing weight. She stopped producing milk, and then eventually her udder started secreting blood. Neither hot and cold compresses nor softened beeswax and warm wraps brought her any relief. The pills that the vet prescribed didn't help any either. "You should have her slaughtered before it's too late," he said after yet another

---

2 Literally "I will take your pain," *tsavd tanem* is a ubiquitous term of endearment in Armenia.

examination, averting his eyes. Khoren almost cursed him out but bit his tongue. If Mushegants Aramais were still alive, he would have figured out a way to save Malishka. This vet is still young; he doesn't know the second thing about life and doesn't think of animals as his equals. And if he doesn't, what good is it to expect him to talk sense?

From that day onward, he took it upon himself to care for his cow and did it with great devotion but without any hope.

"What are we going to do, eh, Malishka?" he would ask, looking her straight in the eyes. She mooed dolefully. Various insects, as if sensing blood, swarmed around her emaciated udder, stinging her painfully and sucking out what meager remnants of vitality she still had, causing her unbearable agony. At first, she tried to drive them off with listless movements of her tail, but eventually she didn't even have enough strength to do that.

She had been born during the worst year of war, when domestic animals were scarce and few. At the sight of her, Maro's daughter-in-law clasped her hands together and swooned, "Oh, what an adorable *malyshka!*"[3] She was of Molokan stock and spoke a singsong dialect of Russian, dragging out the final syllables of her words. "Malishka it is," echoed Khoren.

He had volunteered to drive Maro's daughter-in-law to visit her mother because he knew every inch of the road over the mountain pass. Driving there required a lot of skill—you had to keep changing your speed to make sure the snipers didn't have enough time to take aim. So many years had passed, but he still remembered the crunching sound of the cracks expanding over the windshield and the drawn-out, unexpectedly high-pitched, childlike wailing of her youngest brother: "Katyaaaa! Katyushka?" Khoren had made a U-turn on the

3 Russian term of endearment, literally "baby."

shoulder of the serpentine road because there could have been a trap set up ahead and sped back at lethal speed over the single-lane road that was washed out from the endless rains and was so narrow that two cars couldn't have passed each other. The older brothers, their shoulders pressed against each other, were holding their sister in their arms, while the youngest was steadying the tray with baklava. Two tiny red dots burned, alive, on the linen cloth covering the tray, and he gently caressed them with his forefinger, then thumb, then forefinger again, all the while sobbing like a child.

"What a useless man I've turned out to be, eh, Malishka? I couldn't keep old Maro's daughter-in law safe. I couldn't keep my own daughter, Antaram, safe. And I couldn't even keep you safe from the jackals. What a useless man I've turned out to be," whispered Khoren, stroking the cow's skeletal neck. Malishka breathed heavily from pain but didn't cry. She smelled not of illness but of dew and forget-me-nots. Khoren slaughtered her in the back yard and buried her right there.

When he returned from his sad errand, he found his mother in the shade of the mulberry tree, knitting a child-sized sock.

"Say something to me," he begged.

She smiled in a fleeting and unfocused way, and he ran his fingers over her hand. Her skin was pale, covered in rust-colored dots, and dry like a piece of *lavash*[4] forgotten on the table.

"Say something to me," he implored her.

She finished the row, deftly replaced the purple yarn with the yellow—somehow, in a way fathomable to her alone, she could tell colors apart by touch. Then she lifted her discolored, unseeing eyes to him.

"Look, I am making these striped *gulpa* for my little Khoren. Pretty, aren't they?"

---

4 Armenian flatbread.

Rug

Krnatants Lusine got married on her twentieth birthday. The groom's family came to formally ask for her hand on the first Saturday of September. From her future mother-in-law, she received a ring with a blood-red ruby set in pearl dust, an exquisitely engraved bracelet, and heavy earrings of haughty tarnished gold. The sister-in-law presented her with silk undergarments, the likes of which Lusine had never seen but had secretly coveted: a feather-light nightgown and a dainty garter belt with buttons shaped like butterfly wings. The groom carried in a rug and, for some reason, set it down on the dining table. When the rug was unfolded, everyone gasped. Nani leaned over the armrest of the armchair where she spent all her days. The ninety-year-old woman, who had long lost track of time and events, caressed the rug, listened to the rustling of its pile, ran her rough fingers along its underside and asked, with her lips alone: "Is this one of Antaram's?"

"Yes," came the silent affirmative of the groom's party.

"She's back home at last," Nani's face lit up with joy.

Suffocating from a pain that surged through her, Lusine dropped on her knees and buried her face in Nani's lap. The last time she had seen Nani smile like that was when her youngest great-grandson had miraculously escaped unscathed after flipping over a huge pot of boiling water. That's when she smiled like that, brightly and luminously, and recited a prayer of gratitude.

For a while now, Nani hadn't recognized anyone and lived out her life in reverse. These days, she only saw her children as little kids, not recognizing them in the adults they had become. Lusine would never forget the only time she ever saw her grandfather, Nani's sole son, a mighty, gray-haired old man, invincible and strong, who had never shown uncertainty or doubt, cry; how his shoulders drooped and his face went gaunt and he dissolved into muffled sobs when, in response to him inquiring about her health, his mother responded, guiltily: "I am sorry, I can't recognize you. Who might you be?" To his startled response, "I am your son," she nodded in the direction of her ten-year-old great-grandchild, the same one who had miraculously survived the hot water: "That's my Khoren over there. Who are you?"

Without a shadow of regret, placidly and uncomplainingly, she repudiated her own past, erasing from memory everything that had once constituted her entire reason for living: family, neighbors, her parental home, the summer-singed little alley-ways of old Berd, the cold wind that carried the snowy breath of the mountains on its wings, the damp traces of dew on the *shushaband*[1] window—if you squinted, you could capture sunshine in every glass panel. To her, her children were all little: Khoren was ten, Manishak was eight, Zoya was seven, Zhanna, five. And only her granddaughter, Antaram, was eternally twenty-five.

---

1 In colloquial Armenian, a *shushaband* is a glass-covered veranda or balcony, roughly equivalent to a sunroom.

When the guests left, Lusine took all the ornamental gifts and put them away in a dresser drawer, along with the silk undergarments. Pretty as they were, Lusine would never wear them, except at the wedding so as not to offend her new relatives. She put on a plain cotton dress that smelled comfortingly of wild oregano and hot iron and plaited her hair into a thick braid. She curled up on the rug and pulled its heavy edge over herself. She took a few deep breaths to calm her racing heart and unexpectedly fell asleep. Her slumber was deep and carefree. The rug swaddled her like her mother used to when she was a little girl. And like nobody else ever did.

ANTARAM MADE RUGS. Each one took over a year of work. She had a rare gift for color and proportion. What looked like an uncomplicated pattern in other people's rugs took on life and meaning in hers.

She started when she was twenty and so was relatively late to master the art of rug weaving. In her short lifetime, she only managed to make four rugs. She took the last one to an exhibition in town. There was a lull in hostilities: a ceasefire had just been announced, and the road leading through the mountain pass into the big world had just reopened. But war makes its own rules, and every ceasefire is nothing but an excuse to break it. So Antaram left Berd but never made it into town. The driver's body was found a day later. Antaram had vanished, along with her rug.

Lusine was four at the time, and she didn't remember much from those days. The only thing that remained imprinted in her consciousness was the persistent noxious smell of medication—that was when her Nani's heart gave out. When word reached them that Antaram had been taken hostage, Nani fell into a slumber from which there was no waking. The doctors managed to save her, but she was nearly blind and had no memory of what had happened. She started shedding events and people the way a tree sheds its leaves in autumn.

Antaram was returned to them after time had ticked off an entire winter and half a spring, her body and her arms in two separate bundles. The Azeri word for whore, *qəhbə*, was tattooed on her shaved head. Nani never learned any of this, just as she never learned that from then on, her family would be known as Krnatants, the armless ones.

The only things of Antaram's that the family had left were a loom and a few lifeless balls of yarn. The last rug she had made vanished in the mountains, at the pass. The other three were sold to people who left for faraway places. Nani didn't ask the groom's family by what miracle they had managed to locate the lost rug. She only put her arms around the groom and whispered something into his ear. The groom clenched his teeth and curtly nodded.

Krnatants Lusine got married on her twentieth birthday. The only two things she took from her paternal home were her mother's loom and rug. She hung the rug on the wall and spent countless hours studying its every detail. She shed no tears and spoke no words. Within a year, she learned to weave rugs herself. People called her rugs the Antarams, the never-withering ones. Rumor had it that Lusine wove her mother's name into every rug's pattern. Some folks were able to find it, and others—not.

Valley

T he night spread itself over the world and carefully tucked in the edges of the horizon to keep out every single ray of light and cold draft; then it sprinkled the lower edges of the sky with star dust, muted all sounds, and released the owls and bats to guard the silence. The owls, hooting haughtily, flew through the trees, brushing the branches with the tips of their wide wings. The bats fluttered low enough to make you protectively pull your head into your shoulders—Karen had never forgotten the spooky stories of his childhood about how if a bat attached itself to your face, there would be no prying it off.

"You'll have to live with a bat on your face until it gets old and dies," Lusine would tease him, laughing merrily.

"*Akhchi*,[1] can't you see that you're scaring him? How can you be so little and yet so mean!" his aunt Armenush would come to her nephew's rescue.

Armenush was all of twelve years older than Karen and looked out for him as if he were her little brother. Karen enjoyed her care but nonetheless angrily admonished his aunt, "Who said anything about scared? I just think they're gross."

---

1 Colloquial form of addressing a female, derived from the Armenian word *aghjik*, girl.

He never held a grudge against Lusine because there was
no use holding a grudge against the girl you have decided to
marry! And already back then he was absolutely certain that
he was going to marry her—all he had to do was to grow up.
Maybe in another three years, he thought. At the time, Lusine
had been six, and he—all of nine.

From his surveillance post, he saw the valley laid out below
him. Karen knew every inch of it by heart; even now, in the
almost complete darkness of the night, he could easily make
out the brittle riverbed and the tiny snake of the road stretching
to the foot of Maiden's Cliff and the edge of the abandoned
vineyard, which started right outside Berd and sprawled all the
way to the border: several acres of uncultivated grapevines that
had not been touched by a human hand for almost two decades.

Lusine had come to visit the day before. Of course, she
wasn't permitted into the garrison itself, but Karen was allowed
to spend some alone time with her—we get it, lovebirds, it's
hard to go fifteen days without seeing each other. They held
hands the entire time they were together. Lusine told him
stories about her grandpa, who had to bury his cow, about
her great-grandmother, who had lost her memory and only
remembered her happy days. As always, she didn't say anything
about her mother. Her fingertips had grown rough and her
palms were dyed black—she had spent the previous day peeling
green walnuts for preserves. Furtively looking around to make
sure nobody was watching—otherwise they would have teased
him to death afterward—Karen kissed every single one of her
fingers. Lusine was happy to let him, reassuring him, "Don't
worry, this will wash off soon."

"I don't care if they stay like this!" breathed Karen.

"You'd still love me?"

"I'd still love you."

The sun-soaked valley lay at their feet, generous and placid in a summery way. It made you want to kick off your shoes, fill your lungs with the wind, and race each other from one edge of the valley all the way to the other, to the very border; to hide in the overgrown thickets of grapes and kiss each other to the point of madness, away from everyone's watchful eyes, away from people's attention. Lusine would curl up and press her body to him. He would put one arm around her, and with the other, he would tear off curly grape tendrils and eat them, grimacing from their sour taste.

"Let him lead me to the banquet hall, and let his banner over me be love,"[2] she would whisper, and he would listen, overcome with tenderness. "Like an apple tree among the trees of the forest is my beloved among the young men. I delight to sit in his shade, and his fruit is sweet to my taste,"[3] she would carry on.

"Which fruits of mine did you say would be sweet to your taste?" he would tease her.

She would wriggle free and smack him on the forehead: "You silly goose!"

He would press her to him and say, "You silly hen!"

They wanted to kick off their shoes and race each other along the abandoned vineyard so much that it hurt, but instead they just sat together, holding hands and looking out onto a valley where they had never set foot. They were both children of war and they had internalized its foundational rule: this is our land, that is theirs. The space in between is no man's land, a neutral strip rejected by life itself, and all roads leading to it are closed.

Karen had to stay on his round-the-clock guard-post duty over the valley every other fifteen days: those were the shifts

2 Song of Songs 2:4.

3 Song of Songs 2:3.

that civilian employees of the army served. There were no jobs in the region along the border, especially with the endless flare-ups of hostilities, so all the men ended up going into military service. True, they had to put their lives at risk, but at least they brought home some money. Karen took turns with his dad serving. That's how they lived—the son guarded the border for the first half of each month and the father for the second half. They almost never saw each other, but both could rest assured that their home was looked after in their absence, because the mother and the sisters wouldn't have managed on their own, without a man's help. Dad's younger sister Armenush also needed a hand here and there.

Military service was hard on Karen's father; he had fought in the war and returned home a cripple, with a shattered spine and shrapnel pieces all over his body. Despite the bleak prognoses, he walked again, though the shrapnel in his body still let its presence be felt from time to time. He suffered from the pain but tried not to complain. Instead, he joked, saying, "You'd better make sure I don't get struck by lightning—lightning is a fickle thing; it will hit anything made of metal, and I've got so much metal inside me that if you'd dig all of it out, there'd be enough for a good plow." Only once did Karen see him in a bad mood. It was about two years ago, when Armenush's husband came to visit. Upon learning this, Karen's father had washed up, shaved, showed his wife where he had stashed away their life savings, put on a clean shirt, and set out to kill his good-for-nothing brother-in-law. They had barely stopped him half way.

TOWARD *ENBASHTI*,[4] SILENCE THICKENED over the valley, drowning out the hooting of the owls and the rustling of the wind in the crowns of the centuries-old oak trees, but then

---

4 The witching hour, after midnight, said to possess potential for evil.

the jackals picked up, their howls spreading desperation and anguish everywhere. The jackals had arrived with the war and decided to stay in those parts forever. In the evenings, their distinctive wails spread over the houses, instilling fear in the hearts of the people and the domestic animals alike and whipping the yard dogs into a frenzy—they barked themselves hoarse, trying to break free of their chains. The jackals were part of war; they reeked of it.

The moon glided over the sky, casting its pale radiance. Karen was relieved to observe a hazy nimbus around it, which presaged a milky-white, impenetrable fog that would settle in the morning, giving the villagers a chance to gather their harvest. They could only work in the dead of night or during thick fog because on clear days they made easy targets for the sharpshooters from the other side of the border. Yet another foundational rule of war—the fear inspired by the random killings. The enemy rigorously kept at it, sparing neither the young, nor the women, nor the elderly.

The radio hissed with static. Karen responded and only after switching it off noticed some movement on the right, by the very edge of the vineyard. Peering through his binoculars, he made out a shadow—someone was running toward the border through the neutral territory, not even making much of an effort to hide. There was no time to dawdle. Karen picked up his rifle and took aim; it didn't matter who it was because our people wouldn't be trying to get to the other side, he figured. The shadow collapsed, mowed down by his bullet. Karen was already running as he reported the incident. "Do not abandon your post!" barked the radio, but it was too late; Karen had already covered half the distance between his post and the wounded person.

"Send someone to cover for me," he panted, without slowing down.

"You'd better hope he's still alive," growled the radio, signing off with an angry curse.

The man was motionless, lying face down. Karen kicked him with his boot while keeping his gun trained on him. The man moaned and tried to turn over but failed; he only managed to move his arm, which was bloodied up to the elbow. Karen flipped him onto his back and froze in his tracks—it was a teenager, no older than fourteen, badly beaten up, with bruises and abrasions on his face. Karen examined the wound. His bullet had hit just below the left side of his ribcage; the wound was bleeding profusely but didn't appear to be life-threatening. "Azeri?" he asked. The youth didn't respond but started crying.

The soldiers arrived almost immediately, setting in motion the usual hassle: Karen had to report the incident, explaining in writing why he had disobeyed orders and abandoned his post. Then came the requisite dressing down. The captain, who had known Karen practically since birth, left out nothing, not even Karen's great-grandfather Anes. "Are you as senile as he was? Why the hell did you abandon your post? What if it was a trap? Do you understand that we're at war here?" he thundered. Once he was done with his tirade, he pulled out two cigarettes, one for himself and one for Karen—"Here, have a smoke, dumbass."

They lit up.

"Do you know where this Azeri is from?"

"Negative, sir . . . Captain."

"From Omarbeyli. We can swap him for one of ours. Two, if we're lucky."

Karen, who had only recently picked up smoking, awkwardly twisted the cigarette in his fingers and burned himself. He cast a shy, sideways glance at the captain, who nodded and added, "If we can't exchange him for two of ours, we'll exchange him for one, but under one condition: they have to return the rug even if they have to dig the earth with their noses. We'll get Antaram's rug back. I've given my word, haven't I? We'll get it back."

Waiting

Kolinants Tsovinar was eight when her mother disappeared.

That day, Tsovinar's father had wanted to accompany her mother to town, but she insisted that he should stay, saying she'd be less worried that way. She really did feel more at ease knowing that her mother-in-law, her daughter, and her house would be looked after. Otherwise, who would put away the meticulously washed and fluffed wool for the blankets? Who would warm up and serve the dinner she had prepared before leaving? Her mother-in-law was bedridden with an attack of gout, and Tsovinar, at eight, couldn't manage alone. Her father reluctantly agreed. Around noon, word reached them that the enemy had gained control over the road on the other side of Owl Mountain. Then, that the gun battle began right after the bus transporting her mother had turned toward the mountain pass.

That morning, Tsovinar had been awakened at the crack of dawn by the frantic chirping of sparrows squabbling over their spoils by the basil plants. She went into the kitchen, her bare feet slapping against the cool floor, and returned with a bread crust that she crumbled outside her window. She watched, captivated, as the sparrows immediately dropped their squabble and set upon the crumbs. The tiniest one among them had a few damaged feathers, and Tsovinar wondered if it was hurt. But no, it ate its fill and took off, lively, brushing against the stone wall of the house with its wings. Tsovinar craned her neck and followed its flight as it dove into the morning fog and reemerged, as if for air, before disappearing forever. The dense, viscous fog dissipated slowly and reluctantly, here getting tangled in the branches of an old quince tree, there settling down to rest in the crowns of the oaks. Underneath its opaque cloak, you could make out the outlines of the abandoned vineyard that had grown wild and become overrun with weeds. Untended for decades, the vines had grown out of control, snaking around the posts in layers so thick and heavy as to bend and even break some of them.

Tsovinar's mother was pregnant. She ate and ate insatiably, marveling at how so much food could fit inside a person's body. She was certain that she was having a boy, because when she was pregnant with Tsovinar, she had never felt hungry and had had to make an effort to eat—and the only things she could hold down were bread and cheese. And apples, which she always ate in abundance. Tsovinar's father worshiped the very ground she walked on and denied her nothing. Although, to be fair, she never really asked for much, except for Nemetsants Aleksan's homemade ham. Aleksan's great-grandfather was German, so his smoked meats tasted better than everyone else's; it was not an idle rumor that the Germans were unsurpassed in smoking pork. Lately, her father had to get the ham on credit because his measly salary wasn't enough to buy it. Aleksan never said no to him—"Just pay me back when you can," he'd say.

By the sixth month, her mother's blood pressure started fluc-tuating wildly. The local doctor referred her to a good specialist in town, warning her that she might have to stay on bed rest at the hospital. Her mother waved her hands in protest: "Bed rest? I'll just get some pills and come back!"

Tsovinar walked her to the bus stop. Her mother smiled to her from the bus, looking red-cheeked, round-faced, and content. She unwrapped a piece of chocolate, bit one half off, and offered the other half to her daughter, contorting her entire body to stick her head out of the window because her round belly got in her way.

"No, you have it," Tsovinar shook her head.

Her mom finished the candy and smiled guiltily—she was already hungry.

"You didn't forget to pack your sandwiches, did you?" Tsovinar asked anxiously.

"I have them." Her mother unwrapped the next piece of candy.

GRANDMA GOT OUT OF BED as soon as the terrible news reached them. She put away the wool and swept the yard clean. She mixed the dough for the bread and set it to rise. She worked silently, without grumbling about being in pain. She had always had a strained relationship with her daughter-in-law, and now she tried to make up for every mean word she had ever said during an argument by throwing herself into physical labor that far exceeded her limits. Tsovinar saw how she ran her knotted fingers, mangled by illness, over the pile of sheets that her daughter-in-law had ironed, top to bottom and right to left. Then she pressed her forehead against the sheets and just stood, motionless, for a long time, before putting the laundry away into the linen chest. Every one of her movements—measured, monotonous—looked like a prayer for salvation.

They won back control of the road through the mountain pass on the evening of the very next day. Tsovinar's father immediately set out to search for his wife. He returned gaunt, with extinguished eyes and his face changed beyond recognition. It took Tsovinar a while to figure out what was odd about his appearance—he had more gray hair, which made his eyebrows look unnaturally dark and gave his face a sullen, gloomy expression. He went completely gray by the end of that very week. He soon joined the army and went to serve at the border.

"And every thought was a dream, and every urge was white-hot, and the distance beckoned us out of darkness," were among her father's favorite lines from Teryan.[1] He would talk about forgiveness and the strength of the human spirit in the face of ordeals. Tsovinar remembered those words forever.

Every evening around seven o'clock, Tsovinar packed some provisions: some bread and cheese, a thermos of tea, an apple, and a few pieces of candy. She took these to the bus stop, positioned herself on a bench, and settled down to wait. She knew that if her mom came back, feeding her would be the first order of business, because lately she had been eating as if she had become a different person. She ate so much that Tsovinar's dad would tease her—"What if your bellybutton bursts open?"

"It just might," her mom would retort, helping herself to a third serving of chicken soup.

Time moved slower than a tortoise: June, then July. There was no word from Dad, and Grandma went about her house-work in complete silence. She never told Tsovinar not to go to the bus stop but cried every time the girl left.

Once, a man's cough woke Tsovinar up. She sprinted out of her room and threw her arms around her dad's neck. He had grown skinny and looked disheveled. He was hunched over,

---

1 Vahan Teryan (1885–1920) was an Armenian poet and public activist. The quote is from his poem "Reminiscences about the Lazarevsky Institute."

smoking, the cigarette shielded by his palm. A rifle stood in the corner of the room, pointing at the ceiling and smelling of gunpower and death.

"Come along, I've got something to show you," he said, heading for the door. "Just put on something warm."

Tsovinar pulled the first thing she found out of the closet, threw it over her shoulders, and hurried after him. He paused on the stairs, extinguished his unfinished cigarette against the banister and tossed the butt into the yard. Tsovinar quickly averted her eyes; he never would have done that before.

He pressed on without waiting for her, as if certain that she'd follow, and she did, but she kept asking, "Where are we going?" He walked even faster, without responding, and she ran after him because she suddenly felt afraid that if she lost sight of him, she would never see him again. Her father stopped by the barn door, clanking a heavy key in a padlock. Tsovinar, startled by the sight of a lock on a door that had never been locked before, looked on in silence. She followed him in and stood inside for a while, letting her eyes adjust to the darkness. Once they did, she made out a vague outline of a body in the corner—there was a man lying on the ground. His wrists and legs were tightly bound with rope, his mouth was gagged, and his face was caked with blood.

"It's a hostage," her father said curtly, over his shoulder. "I took him so I can use him for a swap."

Tsovinar's heart was beating out of her chest.

"Mom's been found?"

Her father emitted a dry cough.

"In case she's found."

Tsovinar broke into tears.

Around midday, she peeked into the barn. The bound man was lying on his side, sobbing and breathing with effort.

Worried that he might suffocate, she pulled out his gag. Then she wet her handkerchief and wiped his face. Underneath the crust of blood and dirt, she discovered a young, practically adolescent face.

"Want something to drink?" asked Tsovinar.

The young man shook his head no. She went back to the house, made some tea, put it in the thermos to make sure she wouldn't spill it, and returned to the barn. She poured some into the thermos cup and brought it to his lips, but he pulled back in fright.

"Have some!"

The boy started crying.

"Please, have some," insisted Tsovinar.

The door swung open, and her father materialized in the entrance.

"What are you doing here?"

"I just wanted to give him something to drink," Tsovinar turned to him. "He's refusing though, I think he's afraid that the tea may be poiso . . ."

Her father grabbed her by the shoulder and violently jerked her up into a standing position.

"Whom are you serving tea? Whom?! Are?! You?! Serving?! Tea?!"

His face, terrifying and suddenly foreign, hung over her menacingly, and Tsovinar shut her eyes so she wouldn't have to see this side of her father, a side she never wished to know. The thermos slipped from her fingers, scalding her leg, and rolled to the side.

The door of the barn swung open again.

"Son! Son! What are you doing?" screamed Grandma.

Her father let go of her shoulders and stormed out, angrily

kicking the thermos on his way. It crashed into a wall and shattered with a pitiful crunch.

Tsovinar wiped her tears. Her heart was beating so hard it felt like it would explode. She took a few deep breaths to calm down the hammering inside her chest, picked up the jacket that she'd thrown over her shoulders when she had rushed out of the house, put it on, aimlessly felt inside the pockets and discovered a piece of candy. She unwrapped it and bit off a piece. She swallowed it, too agitated to taste it. Then she approached the hostage.

"See, it's not poisoned."

She brought the candy to his lips. He gulped it down.

He smelled of sweat and human excrement, and his tightly bound wrists and legs were bleeding where the ties had cut into his skin. Tsovinar wanted to loosen the rope, but her grandma wouldn't allow it; she only helped him up into a seated position, with his back leaning against the wall. She instructed her granddaughter to bring warm water, soap, and the old kitchen towels she had set aside to be used as rags.

Tsovinar's father was gone. The rifle was gone, too, but it had left an untidy dark smudge on the whitewashed wall. Tsovinar wet her finger with her spit and tried to wipe it off, but she only made it worse.

In the evening, she took another peek inside the barn. The boy was sleeping, his head resting on his chest. She woke him up and gave him tea. He lifted his eyes and wanted to ask her something but stopped short, too afraid to continue.

"Go on, don't worry," she encouraged him.

Grandma waited until nightfall, cut his ropes, and led him out to the abandoned vineyard, pointing him in the right direction. He kissed her hand and vanished into the darkness.

They could hear him making his way through the brush for a few minutes, and then silence fell.

The next evening, Tsovinar prepared provisions: some bread and cheese, the requisite handful of candy and an apple. At a quarter to seven, she was already sitting on the bench at the bus stop with the bundle of food balanced on her knees, waiting for her mom.

Summer

Pel-Anesants Armenush has five daughters, between the ages of seven and sixteen.

Pel-Anesants Armenush has a cow named Kosulia, a nanny goat named Tilo, and a dog named Valet. Then there is her entire henhouse full of domestic fowl: nameless guinea fowl along with the usual lineup of geese, chickens, and pheasants. There is also a turkey named Dushman[1]—a thug and a terrorist who rules the entire neighborhood with fear. Armenush doesn't know what to do with him; he's incorrigible and a hundred times more aggressive than the guard dog. Valet whimpers guiltily and covers his muzzle with his paws. Unlike the turkey, the dog is a Good Samaritan whose entire attitude projects hospitality: be my guest, enter the house, help yourself to anything you'd like, no need to bring it back. Dushman, by contrast, looks like the harbinger of apocalypse: disheveled and ferocious, with two different-colored eyes. He is fat and clubfooted but surprisingly nimble and can reach ground speeds of seventy-five miles per hour. Dushman rams his way through whatever he encounters, regardless of what it may be. Every unexpected guest is his sworn enemy. He rushes at

---

1 "Enemy" or "fiend" in Turkish and Farsi, a word commonly used in Armenian as well.

them, gobbling furiously and trying to chase them out the gate. Just recently, guests from town had come in a black car to visit Armenush's neighbors. Dushman spotted his reflection in the car's polished side, deemed his own reflection his foe, and wore himself out attacking it. His failure to vanquish the enemy infuriated him so much that he tore out a wad of feathers from his own chest.

Afterward, Armenush excoriated him: "You are embarrassing us in front of everyone. You should be ashamed of yourself!"

Dushman was silent, his beak twisted in a contemptuous smirk.

"Fine then, suit yourself, walk around scruffy and with bald patches on your chest."

"A-gobble-gobble-gobble-gobble!"

"*Zahrumar!*[2] You're the one who made a fool of yourself, and you're the one arguing!"

Every morning in Armenush's life resembles all the others, just as every evening repeats the preceding one. As does the next one. Milk the cow and the nanny goat and send them out to pasture with the herd. Give feed to the fowl. Weed and water the garden. Boil the day's milk. Use some of it for cream and butter, and the rest for different kinds of fresh cheese. Mix the dough for the bread. Prod the younger daughters to clean up their room. Start the stove. Set the breakfast table. Make sure one of the girls washes the dishes because they'll never do it voluntarily—they all try to avoid housework. Bake some *gata*[3] with walnut filling, let it cool, and arrange it in

---

2 While the word has a number of meanings in Armenian associated with bitterness, noxiousness, and poison, it is usually used to express consternation and disapproval, akin to the English expression "go to hell."

3 A traditional Armenian dessert made of flaky dough rolled up with sweet filling.

a wicker basket. Send the older girls to the market to sell it. Around noon, when the sun, hotter than the stove, perches at the highest point in the sky, hang the laundry to dry and finally rest for a minute. After this brief respite starts the new round: ironing, cooking, sewing, and darning. Wait for the older girls to return from the market, set the supper table. Herd the chickens back into the henhouse, chiding Dushman along the way. Meet the herd. Milk the cow and the goat. Use some of the milk to make yogurt, store the rest of it in the cold cellar. Remember to say good night to Valet. Make sure the girls bathe themselves and dry their hair. Plait their braids. Bless them before they go to sleep.

At night, when the moon finally peeks from behind the shoulder of Khali-Kar, casting its timid rays over the hushed world, Armenush turns down the lights, lights an oil lamp, and makes herself some thyme tea. She spreads out sheets of paper on the table and rereads whatever she has written the day before with a critical eye, crossing out entire sentences and paragraphs. Then she copies out the rest on a clean sheet of paper and picks up where she left off:

"... *of eternal spring. Of sunbaked rooftops. Of the cicadas' incessant song pouring from the palm of one's hand into a hot summer afternoon. Of the birds' chirping and late sunsets. Of the dense sky hanging low overhead at night—so low that all you need to do is stand on your tiptoes and you can scoop entire handfuls of its bilberry-colored milk. Of the wind rustling in the crowns of the oak trees the way that only the wind can—as if breathing: hrrrsh, hrrrsh, hrrrsh . . .*"

Armenush falls asleep long after midnight and wakes up at the crack of dawn.

"Maybe Dad will come visit us today?" asks her youngest daughter over breakfast.

"Maybe he will," Armenush says.

The older girls exchange meaningful glances and snort, but then fall silent, checked by their mother's eyes. It's been two years since they last saw their father. He came for a week and left again.

True, he diligently sends them money. It's not a lot, but still. Sometimes he phones. "My dear daughters, my dear daughters." The younger ones are eager to chat with him, but the older ones will curtly say hello before passing the receiver on to their siblings. Armenush reasons with them: "Talk to him. He is your father, your blood, your protector, and your pillar of support." The older daughters find this annoying: "What kind of a protector is he? There's more use in Dushman than him! Even Valet does more for us!"

"They've grown up, it's hard to handle them," Armenush later confides in her neighbor Nunik.

"Well, what did you expect? They are big girls, they understand everything," retorts Nunik.

"A father is to be loved, not understood," objects Armenush.

"It's enough that *you* love him!"

"I'm not even sure if I do love him."

"Of course you do! He was out chasing skirts while you were bearing him children. You'd probably have another kid if he ever came to visit."

Armenush sighs.

All she had heard since childhood was that sacrifice was the most important part of love. You're an Armenian woman, and therefore you must give yourself fully to the ones you love: your parents, your husband, your children. They all come before you—that's what love means.

She gave herself as much as she had the strength to: she worshiped her parents, she selflessly loved her children and her numerous nieces and nephews, she devotedly cared for her gravely wounded husband whose recovery was slow, halting, and filled with nightmares. As soon as he fell asleep, he'd wake up again, in sweat and tears. When he finally did recover, he took to chasing skirts. Perhaps that was his attempt to escape death, or perhaps he had missed living to the fullest. After every short-lived affair, he returned home and begged her on his knees to forgive him, swearing never to do it again. She believed him and bore him yet another child. Then he would disappear again. Eventually, he left for good. Armenush didn't spend the measly sums of money he sent home. She put all of it away into a box. She managed on her own—she baked, sewed, and knitted things to sell, and didn't shy away from taking on backbreaking work: she washed other people's rugs, feathers, and sheep's wool, stuffed and stitched the heavy village-style blankets, made pillows, helped with harvesting and preparing winter preserves. She was constantly in motion, like a hamster in a wheel, but she managed to make ends meet somehow. When her older daughters confronted her about why she refused to spend the money their father had sent, she'd just shrug and say, "Leave it alone for now, we'll see about it later."

". . . *of eternal summer. Of thunderstorms, sudden and short-lived, with their metallic rattling against drainpipes. Of lightning, the kind you only see in the mountains, with five tips, each deadly like the spear of a heavenly azhdahak*[4] *piercing the earth. Of going out onto the veranda in the middle of a thunderstorm unafraid, because lightning does not strike those who don't fear it, to step, barefoot, over the floorboards, breathing: hrrsh, hrrsh, hrrsh . . .*"

The people of Berd think Armenush is a holy fool. They say she takes after her great-grandfather, Anes, whose senility

---

4 In Armenian mythology, an evil man-dragon, or a giant.

earned him the nickname Pel, which means fool. He refused
to let people pay him back money they had borrowed from
him. You need the money more than me, he'd say. He lived
modestly, practically in poverty. He was an odd man, touched
by God. He made up wondrous, outlandish tales about blind
sea monsters that fed on human sin and therefore never saw
daylight, about the bird of peace that had spent five thousand
years in the sky, unable to come down to earth because it could
only land where there was no war. And there was war everywhere on earth.

Pel-Anesants Armenush has definitely taken after her
great-grandfather, insist the people of Berd. She has hoisted
the entire world on her shoulders and insists on carrying it: her
daughters, her home, her homestead. She even sticks up for
her good-for-nothing husband. Rumor has it, he is living the
good life in town and only sends home those meager pennies
so people won't say he has abandoned his family. Anyone else
would have sued him for alimony, but Armenush loves him and
keeps waiting for him to come home. She even chides her older
daughters when they refuse to talk to their father.

"Pride! You've got to have some pride!" her neighbor Nunik
explodes, unable to keep her cool.

"I am a happy person, what do I need pride for?" asks
Armenush.

"What do you mean, happy?" the neighbor's voice cracks
with indignation.

Armenush doesn't argue with her.

"You are still young and pretty—you're only thirty-six.
How do you picture the rest of your life?" the neighbor carries
on, annoyed.

"I picture it clearly. First, I'll get my daughters through
school and marry them off. Then I'll take care of my grandkids.

God willing, there will be a bunch of them. I have so much love in me, there's enough for everyone."

Dushman gobbles furiously, staring with his bicolored eyes through a crack in the fence. He is upset that Armenush has gone to visit the neighbors and hasn't taken him along. What if someone tries to hurt her?

"A-gobble-gobble-gobble-gobble!" he grumbles. When his grumbling goes unanswered, he runs at the fence and slams into it with the bald spot on his chest.

"I better get going before he kills himself," Armenush giggles guiltily.

"Do you ever dream of anything?" Nunik refuses to end the conversation.

Pel-Anesants Armenush brushes the hair off her forehead and smiles pensively.

"Do I dream? I do. Of eternal summer."

"*. . . of eternal summer. Of walking around the streets, gathering people's smiles like daisies. Every smile contains a piece of the sun. Handfuls of the sun. Everybody is generous, everybody shares. I am not crying, I simply go around gathering the smiles. It's not hard, I can manage!*"

Prayer

I t's been years since Safarants Nunik has set foot outside her yard. Ever since the day she returned from her brother's funeral to discover a smoking crater instead of her two-story stone house and her orchard of fruit trees, she has never stepped outside her gate. The house couldn't be rebuilt—it would be like reconstructing a loaf of crumbled cornbread, thought Nunik apathetically, as she turned over pieces of charred stone in her hands. She had no tears—she had cried them out at the funeral. Her brother was forty-two: young, strong, handsome, but foolhardy and stubborn—come to think of it, much like all the other men of the Safarants clan. He worked as a bus driver and transported people from wartime Berd to the big world that lay beyond it. After a bus full of passengers went missing at the treacherous mountain pass, Nunik literally threw herself at his feet, begging him to quit his job. He shrugged his shoulders: "Who'll transport the people if I quit?"

"Someone else," Nunik snapped. "You have a family and kids to think about."

"Oh, so other people don't have families and kids to think about?" her brother caustically repeated her words, and added, annoyed, "Can *you*, at least, quit nagging me? As it is, my wife has practically drilled a hole in my bald spot with her nagging."

"We do it out of love! We are just worried about you," sobbed Nunik, at once closing ranks with her sister-in-law, whom she couldn't stand for her narrow-mindedness and her penchant for idle chatter. Her brother laughed then and kissed her on the temple, but firmly asked that she stop bothering him with such requests. Nunik said nothing and never had the courage to raise the topic again. She prayed for her brother the best she could: "Astvats-jan,[1] save and protect him, you know that he's all I've got in this world." Astvats listened in silence, and there was no knowing whether he heard her or not. But Nunik didn't let this discourage her. She went to church and lit candles for her brother's health and long life. She always saved the biggest candle for the icon of the Virgin Mary, Mariam Astvatsatsin—"At least *you* don't leave my pleas unanswered, please!"

Nunik often performed a *matagh*,[2] scrupulously making sure that it never fell on a Wednesday, a Friday, or a fasting day. She looked after her cockerels like they were the apple of her eye and didn't slaughter them in the autumn, as others did. People usually leave the strongest and feistiest cockerel for the henhouse and use the rest for food because they aren't good for anything; they don't lay or hatch eggs, they only waste feed and crow at the top of their lungs for no good reason. But Nunik saved up her cockerels for the *mataghs*, since only the male birds could be sacrificed. The ritual also

---

1 *Astvats* in Armenian means "God"; *jan* is a colloquial term of endearment used with family and friends. Literally, the phrase means "Dear God."

2 A tradition of animal sacrifice still practiced in the Armenian Orthodox Church. It is guided by strict rules about acceptable days for the sacrifice, the gender of the sacrificial animal (only males may be sacrificed), the preparation of the slaughtered animal, and even the disposal of its bones.

demanded that a man do the actual slaughtering, so she would
arrange with Binoyants Grigor, who, ever since returning
from the North,[3] never turned down anyone's request for
help and generally tried to make himself useful. Grigor not
only slaughtered the cockerel but, over Nunik's objections,
cleaned it as well: he scalded the bird in boiling water and
meticulously plucked its feathers, careful not to damage the
skin. After washing the bird's body, he gutted it: he made a
neat incision from the tail to the breastbone, carefully removed
the guts, making sure not to puncture the gallbladder, then
washed out any remaining bits from the cavity. He performed
all of this in complete silence. If Nunik asked questions, he
sometimes answered in monosyllables, but for the most part he
limited himself to either nodding yes or shaking his head no.
Nunik didn't feel slighted by his silence. She stood watching
him for a few minutes and then went to make him coffee,
coming back with a steaming cup balanced on a saucer with
a piece of pastry. Grigor drank the coffee but never touched
the sweets.

Nunik then boiled the bird in water seasoned with church-
blessed salt, cut it into seven pieces and, having arranged
the portions on a tray and covered them with a linen cloth,
distributed them to seven households, as the ritual demanded.
She used red silk ribbon to tie up the head and the feet of the
sacrificed cockerel and hung them from the sacrificial tree to
ward off evil. Then she addressed the heavens: "Astvats-jan,
as you are my witness, I have done everything that was in my
power. The rest is in your hands."

---

3 After the collapse of the Soviet Union and the establishment of the independent
Armenian state, many Armenian men left Armenia to work as migrant workers in
Russia, driven both by the dire economic situation in Armenia and by a desire to
escape mandatory military service.

Her brother died during the dog days of summer. Hit by a projectile, the compact PAZ bus[4] he was driving tumbled into the gorge, taking eighteen lives with it. Only Levon, the youngest son of Zarginants Atanes, made it out alive, because he was thrown through a window onto the side of the road by the explosion.

News of her brother's death reached Nunik when she was hard at work baking bread. They told her later that when she heard about what had happened, she silently finished kneading the dough, covered it with a linen napkin to keep it from drying, washed her hands, meticulously dried them with a towel, and then fainted. She remembered none of this. When she came to, she was ill, her eyes dull and her hands beset by a tremor. Her health slowly recovered but the trembling in her hands never went away. Normally, it was unnoticeable, but when Nunik became agitated, her hands were overcome with such spasms that she had to cross her arms over her chest to steady them. She went to her brother's funeral with a monstrous headache—she had a migraine attack. A brief shelling broke out during the ceremony, with a few projectiles exploding behind them in the distance, but nobody even turned around to see where they had hit. Upon returning from the cemetery, Nunik discovered smoldering ruins in the spot where her house had stood.

"Your brother saved your life," observed one of her neighbors. "If you hadn't gone to the funeral, you . . ."

"It would have been better if I had stayed home," Nunik nipped the conversation in the bud.

---

4 Small buses used mostly for regional transportation on low-demand routes. First produced in the 1960s, they remain in wide use in the countries of the former Soviet Union.

After that, she never left the confines of her yard. For some reason, she had decided that death would come to collect her right there, of all places. "I cheated death once, but I won't do it the second time!" she declared to her sister-in-law. The latter was about to cry but quickly wiped her tears because she didn't want to upset Nunik. These days, she dropped in frequently, as if for a casual visit, and sent the kids to check in on her as well. Nunik knew she was doing it out of fear—she was afraid that Nunik would do the unconscionable. To this, Nunik just shrugged her shoulders, baffled; if she had wanted to take her own life, she would have done it a long time ago.

Binoyants Grigor helped her build a tiny hut with two rooms, and the neighbors came through with housewares. Armenush stopped by once a week to get the list of things that Nunik needed. Day in and day out, Nunik sewed and knitted—she had tons of orders both in her native Khanlar and in Berd, where she had moved with her brother during the war. Her mother had refused to leave with them. She stayed back to guard the house and their possessions, saying, "Someday, the war will end and you'll come back." She brushed off their attempts to change her mind: "I am Assyrian, they won't touch me."

"Mom, you see what's going on," cried Nunik.

Her mom refused to yield: "I'm so old, nobody would raise a hand against me."

She was wrong, as it turned out; she wasn't too old for someone to raise a hand against her after all. She was stuffed into a truck tire, like a rag doll, and burned alive.

In her mind, Nunik frequently pictured the world where her brother and mother now resided. There, the river Giandjay flows; there, in stone-walled cellars, sweet wine ages; there, translucent persimmons, the final gifts of the departing sun,

ripen on cellar shelves; there, with characteristic restraint,
toll the bells of the *Kirche*[5]—during the Second World War,
all the Germans were resettled to Kazakhstan, but the *Kirche*
was never torn down, and so it stood silently, with boarded-up
doors and windows. The only road leading to that blessed world
is overgrown with blackberry bushes, and mighty plantain
trees, bent by endlessly blowing wind, have put their crowns
together in a canopy, forming a shaded alley.

Nunik knew for certain that someday she would join them
in that world. She awaited her day patiently and with grace.
She didn't rush the time; nor did she needlessly cling to
life. Sometimes, as she followed the flight of a falcon, a rare
sighting in these parts, she froze for a moment, looking up as if
in anticipation of some sign before lowering her eyes. She never
again bothered God with any requests.

---

5 German for "church," the word is used to refer specifically to small Lutheran
churches built by German immigrants living in the region.

Homecoming

Binoyants Grigor was coming home. The intercity bus, its engine howling angrily, covered turn after turn on the serpentine road through the mountain pass. The broad-legged wooden cross was swaying on the windshield, and Grigor had to turn away to conceal his smile from the driver: when living abroad, Grigor could always tell his compatriots by those crosses. Onik loved to crack jokes on that account.

"If they could, they'd take the mountains with them too," he liked to repeat. "It's like they try to take everything with them when they leave: from the familiar window view to their ancestors' tombstones. You get into a car like this and you get a feeling that if you turn around you might find Mount Ararat in the back seat."

Grigor would listen silently, without contradicting him. Onik was accustomed to his silence, so he both asked the questions and answered them.

"Have you ever thought what a strange nation we are? A snail nation." And, noticing his friend's puzzled expression, he offered up a clarification: "I mean that in a good sense; we carry everything with us."

BINOYANTS GRIGOR WAS COMING HOME. The road was
long, almost endless. The desolate and abandoned forest
stretched on the right side; November was drawing to an end,
and soon it would be winter. On the left was the steep slope
of Maiden's Cliff, mottled with whitish scars from the rapid
and deadly mudflows that rushed with a terrifying roar into
the bottomless abyss of Khuzani-Kar every God-given spring.
It was twelve years ago that one of those very mudflows had
saved their lives. The war was on, it was a long day of battle,
they had almost no bullets left, and there was neither any hope
for help nor any place to retreat, because behind them was
their native Berd. Onik even wryly chuckled, "We can't even
shoot ourselves, because who'll take care of it?" And just then
the mudflow erupted; with a frozen wave, as if with a razor, it
clipped the ledge of the cliff from where they were being shot
at, and, passing no more than half a yard away from them,
disappeared into the abyss.

They got baptized the same day. Ter Vartan[1] dispensed with
all the ceremonies, just hurriedly read the prayer and drew a
cross on both of their foreheads. When he came out to have a
smoke with them afterward, he couldn't resist asking sarcasti-
cally, "You couldn't have come during peacetime?"

"Be grateful we came at all!" Onik retorted.

Ter Vartan just waved his hand at them: "I guess I didn't
pound you hard enough when we were at school."

"Not nearly enough!" agreed Grigor.

Ter Vartan was gone within a week, killed by shrapnel in his
chapel's courtyard. Where once there were three friends, now
only two remained.

---

1 *Ter* is a title indicating a member of the clergy.

BINOYANTS GRIGOR WAS COMING HOME. Only his closest family came to pick him up in town: his wife, his parents, Ter Vartan's widow, and Onik's wife Manana with her son.

His father's blood pressure spiked at the airport; he got too agitated when the flight was delayed. His mother cried the whole way there and calmed down only once she saw her son. She hugged him, pressing her body against his chest,

"I will never let you go anywhere again!"

"I don't intend to," Grigor replied simply.

"Where is he?" mouthed Manana.

He handed the heavy urn not to her but to her son. The boy blinked but held his tears at bay.

When they were getting into the car, they realized that there was no room for Grigor.

"I don't understand. Everybody fit on the way here," said his father.

"Well, did you count me?" asked Grigor.

His father froze, his mouth agape.

"I'll take the bus, there is one leaving pretty soon," Onik's son volunteered.

"I'll take it," declared Grigor in a voice that left no room for further discussion, adding quietly, "You'd better stay with your mom."

They proceeded in a convoy: the bus drove ahead, followed by his father's car. Next to his father sat Manana, pressing the urn to her chest and wiping her eyes with her fingers. Every time the bus made a right turn, Grigor saw her tear-stained face in the side window.

THEY WORKED HARD, in three shifts and without breaks. Sometimes they dreamed, naively, in a childlike way, that one day they would get rich, return home, and open a canning factory. They would produce all the local delicacies: walnut and dogwood jam, wild plum and pear compotes, fire-roasted vegetable ragout, and real *ghaurma*[2] made with the purest mountain butter.

"I will be the director and you will be deputy director," Onik would declare, adding in anticipation of any questions: "A silent director is the undoing of any business."

"But a chatty one is its salvation, right?" Grigor would contradict resentfully.

"A chatty one is the guarantee of success."

When Grigor wanted to tease his friend, he'd call him just that: "the guarantee of success." Onik didn't take it personally. One day he left to get the merchandise and did not come back. They found out about the crash and the fire that completely burned the car only the next morning.

Onik always said that he would live for one hundred years and a day. "I will live till I meet my first great-great-grandchild, and then we'll see how the dice roll." This is how the dice rolled: once there were three friends, now only one remained.

They had left Maiden's Cliff behind; soon they'd be passing by the reservoir, and then Berd would appear, with the tops of its centenarian cypresses propping up the sky.

Binoyants Grigor brought back everything he had taken with him when he left for faraway lands: the familiar view from the window, the gravestones of his ancestors, Ararat (Major and Minor), his unfulfilled dreams, and the unbearable burden of being. Binoyants Grigor was coming home.

---

2 Slow-cooked beef covered with melted butter and kept in a cold cellar.

A Toast

Nobody can help smiling when they see Nugzar: fiery red hair, huge green eyes, a hooked, broken nose recklessly hanging over his upper lip. To cover his bald spot, he does a comb-over from ear to ear. If the wind blows in the wrong direction, the carefully slicked comb-over spreads out like a fan. Nugzar catches it and smooths it down with his fingers. His face turns so fiery red that it seems like it may catch fire any second now.

Nugzar has too many freckles to count. Each one is the size of a southern broad-leaved sunflower. During the summer, when the sun unleashes peoples' freckles, Nugzar turns into a blooming field of sunflowers. He gets sunburned decisively and irrevocably: red, funny, ginger-haired. His brother, making fun of his hirsuteness, used to say that if you sheared Nugzar, you'd get enough hair to knit an entire human sweater.

"If I hadn't gone bald, you'd get two," Nugzar would add.

On weekends, he stops by the church. He helps with the chores: some repairs, taking out the trash. His first time there, the old women shook their heads and eagerly tried to explain that his way of crossing himself was incorrect: it had to be done not from right to left, but from left to right. When they realized that he was Eastern Orthodox, they made zealously sure that he did not get confused: with everyone crossing themselves from left to right, what if he got distracted and repeated after them? What if the Georgian God took offense? One never knows what goes on in the heads of these gods! Nugzar buried his face in his freckled hands and laughed so hard that his whole body shook.

"*Vaime*,[1] what kind of people are you?"

"What did you think?" the old ladies haughtily clucked.

Nugzar lives with his sister Manana. Manana has two sons and a blind father-in-law, Kazinants Oganes. Sometimes Nugzar takes him out for a stroll. If Nugzar sees someone he knows, he warns Oganes, "Look, Avakants Mishik is coming this way."

"Hello, Mishik-jan," Oganes greets him.

"Hello, Oganes-api." Mishik shakes hands, first with the old man, then with Nugzar. He respects seniority. They part after some small talk, but not before another round of handshakes.

Holding him by the elbow, Nugzar leads Oganes and updates him on the most recent Berd news.

"Ankhatants Varuzh just had his third child."

"A son?" Oganes tries to clarify.

"Quite the opposite," diplomatically counters Nugzar.

"Someone's jinxed him, that's for sure. A third girl—that's no joke. Something needs to be done about this!"

"What is there to do?"

"What do you mean? Remove the jinx!"

"*Vaime!*" gasps Nugzar.

The world is large, while Berd is tiny, no bigger than a pinhead. However, people from the large world sometimes pop

---

1 Generic Georgian exclamation, roughly equivalent to "wow."

up even there. Just recently, some Frenchmen and Norwegians came to visit. Manana teaches English at the school, which is why all the foreigners are taken to her. Nugzar starts a fire in the courtyard. While the meat is roasting over the coals, he helps his sister set the table and brings the hooch out of the cellar. The guests quickly grow tipsy from all the food and drink. They pepper their conversations with jokes. At the height of all the merriment Manana's father-in-law stands up at the head of the table and asks for silence.

"Batono Oganes,[2] please don't!" implores Nugzar.

Oganes stops him with a gesture, turns to Manana (blind as he is, he unfailingly knows where his daughter-in-law is), and says: "Translate."

Manana assumes her position on his left. The guests fall silent. Nugzar leaves the room, tightly closing the door behind himself. Oganes raises his glass. He talks slowly, with dignity, looking ahead with his unseeing eyes: "I want to offer this toast for Nugzar, the brother of Manana, my daughter-in-law. I have not seen him for five years now, ever since I went blind. I hope he has not changed much. Manana, has he changed much?"

"Not really," Manana assures him. "He still has ginger hair and freckles."

"He looks a bit like Gérard Depardieu, the actor," jokes one of the guests.

"Perhaps he does," says Oganes. "Perhaps he doesn't. It so happened that Manana and I were bereaved: I lost my son, she lost her husband, and my grandchildren lost their father. Now Nugzar takes care of us. He is the most easygoing person I have ever known. Although his life hasn't been easy at all."

Oganes switches the hand holding the shot glass and puts his arm around his daughter-in-law. Manana lowers her head.

2 Respectful form of address in Georgian. *Batono* literally means "master."

The guests grow quiet and sit expectantly. An oppressive silence hangs over the room. Oganes tries to continue but words get stuck in his throat. He coughs once, then again. But he cannot pronounce a single word. He gives up with a bitter smirk.

"To our Nugzar!" He downs his shot in one gulp and slowly leaves the room.

The guests look at each other: what an odd old man—he wanted to tell us a story but changed his mind. Engaged in conversation, they soon forget about him. Manana changes their plates: the *khashlama*[3] is almost ready to be served.

KAZINANTS OGANES WALKS DOWN the hallway, clinging to the wall. Thirty steps ahead, he pushes the door and turns left, then another ten steps, then left again. He walks out onto the veranda and all the way to its farthest corner. Takes a cigarette from Nugzar, inhales deeply.

A rooster is perched on the fence, watching the world—now with one, now with the other yellow eye. Displeased with what he sees, he crows as if squabbling.

"Do you know how roosters sound in our language?" Oganes asks and immediately answers, "Tsugh-ru-ghu."

"In ours, they go 'kee-kli-ko.'"

"You Georgians can't do anything right."

"Of course, while you Armenians do everything right, don't you? Think before you talk!" Nugzar counters with a quotation from his favorite movie.[4]

After sharing a good laugh, they fall silent. They stay silent for a very, very long time. They do not mention that once there

---

3 A dish made from braised meat (beef or lamb), onions, tomatoes, and bell peppers.

4 The movie is *Mimino*, a 1977 film directed by Georgi Danelia, a comedy about how an Armenian and a Georgian become fast friends in Moscow but also constantly compete to prove that their nation is better.

was a war in Nugzar's village. Or that people, forced to leave their village, opened the barns and the rabbit cages so the animals wouldn't starve to death. Or that they left the doors of their houses wide open so the new, uninvited masters would not break them in. Come in, make yourselves at home, just don't destroy things.

They say nothing about how Nugzar was trying to find his way to the border through a gloomy, impassable forest, because on the roads the refugees were robbed and killed. They say nothing about how he carried on his back the corpse of his brother: he could not leave him behind. His brother was ordered to put down the package that he was taking from his paternal home as he was leaving it for good. "Drop it," they said, shoving the butt of a rifle into his ribs. He refused, and they shot him dead on the spot. When he fell, the package split open, and family pictures spilled out on the floor: Georgian grandpas and grandmas, acacias in the botanical garden, a hot seashore.

Nugzar lifted his brother onto his shoulders and carried him for three days, through the forest, through the fields, through the river, so that he could bury him somewhere where he could visit later, to keep his memory alive. He arrived at his sister's in mismatched socks, with a bunch of wild daisies he had picked along the way: he had been raised never to visit people empty-handed, and he had spent his last money on his journey.

Oganes wants to tell that story every time they have guests, but he can't.

Nugzar teaches phys ed at school. Behind his back, children call him *arj*, which means "bear." He does indeed resemble a bear: big, awkward, clubfooted. He breathes as loudly as normal people snore. His pupils love him but often skip his classes. Nugzar never scolds them: What is the point? They are still little, their brains impressionable, not fully formed. You can teach them what you like: if you teach them kindness, they will be kind; if you teach them evil, they will be mean-spirited.

Four times a year he and Manana travel north to the Georgian border, all the way to the river. On this side it is their land, on the other—used to be theirs but is foreign now.

On their brother's grave, mountain irises bloom, delicately purple, airy. Hello, *dzamiko*,[5] here we are. Here we are.

---

5 "Little brother" in Georgian.

Khachkar

O ver the course of centuries, Old Berd's *khachkar*[1] sank to its very midpoint into the ground, slumped, and became overgrown with rufous moss. Nobody had any idea or even solid guess about its true age. Nobody knew of its existence until an earthquake struck in the century before last, taking down a part of the fortification wall dating back to the Middle Ages along with the side of Khali-Kar that used to block the riverbed, collecting its waters into a shallow, clear lake. That's when the *khachkar* was discovered: it was standing all alone in the crevice between two cliffs, unharmed and inaccessible, shielded on all sides against the winds and enemy arrows, and the cross on it was simple and plain, etched at random by the unskilled hand of someone who couldn't possibly have comprehended the significance of his message to posterity.

The inhabitants of Berd rarely make it out to visit the *khachkar*: it makes no sense to travel that far, and it's better to visit the chapel, which is not only closer but also offers shelter in inclement weather. But Avakants Mishik visits the *khachkar* every week. He begins his preparations just after midday, entrusting his grocery store to the thirteen-year-old tailor's apprentice, Masis. Masis, albeit a quick-witted fellow, is not

---

1 Cross-stone.

very good at selling things, so Mishik tries to visit the *khachkar* on Tuesdays—for some reason that's when the grocery store has the fewest customers. Before he leaves, he grinds up some good coffee and pours it into a paper bag. He meticulously selects dried fruit: raisins, dates, and prunes. He gathers fistfuls of chocolate candy, always with a variety of fillings. He packs everything into a shopping bag and wishes Masis a good day.

"Don't worry, I can handle this," the latter reassures Mishik at parting.

"If I thought you couldn't, I wouldn't be leaving the store for you to manage!" responds Mishik.

It takes a little over an hour to get to the *khachkar*. Avakants Mishik takes significantly longer to make the trip. His stride is slow and stately, and he observes Berd with cheerful curiosity, noticing the smallest changes in its appearance: here a branch has broken off a plum tree and is hanging, clinging with its lifeless fingers to the edge of the picket fence; there some ducks are fussing, fighting over a morsel they can't share and arguing in angry quacks. Should he scatter them or not? No, let them figure it out on their own.

Mishik eagerly greets every passerby, asking them in detail about their health, expressing interest in their recent news, and telling them about his own.

"Batono Nugzar, I watched a medical program on TV. They say there is a new eye surgery, a complicated one, but it works. Maybe it will help Oganes too."

"Why do I need a complicated surgery? What can I possibly see in this world that I haven't seen before?" Oganes responds touchily without waiting for Nugzar's response.

"I can see that you're in excellent spirits today, Oganes-keri!"[2] counters Mishik.

---

2 *Keri* means "uncle" in Armenian.

"Insightful as ever!" old Oganes parries the jab.

"I've learned from the best!"

"Ah, you little cur!"

"Wow, what kind of people are you!" Nugzar interrupts their comic banter.

"We live for this!"

They part ways, immensely content with one another.

Didevants Ambo's granddaughter is walking along the edge of the sidewalk, kicking a little pebble with the tip of her shoe and humming to herself.

"Are you returning from work, Yepimeh-jan?" asks Mishik in lieu of a greeting.

"Uh-huh," confirms Yepimeh.

"Look at that pretty butterfly sitting on your shoulder. Watch out, it may take you along when it flies away!"

Yepimeh laughs, covering her mouth with her little palm. Mishik smooths her shiny hair.

"How is your grandpa? Is he better? Is he walking now?"

"Uh-huh."

"Eh, Yepimeh-jan. Such a big girl and still 'uh-huh'-ing like a child."

THE PATH LEADING TO the *khachkar* is narrow and rugged, like the line of life on a person's palm. On either side, inaccessible cliffs rise like stony guards, staring sternly and implacably with the dark eye sockets of their caves. They allow passage only to those who come bearing peace. At the center of the biggest cliff there is a gaping hole in the shape of a torn-out heart—Giants' Cave, a haven for the giants who lived there in times of yore. Mishik used to escape there as a kid, climbing the oddly shaped stone steps, worn down as if the giants had walked there for centuries, leaving behind their giant footprints. For some reason the cave smelled of bitter tobacco smoke and freshly brewed thyme tea. Mishik used to search all the corners of the cave looking for the source of this smell, but eventually he got used to it and gave up. He used to spend long hours sitting at the mouth of the cave, his feet dangling over the abyss, holding his breath. "If you can sit like that for three hundred heartbeats and not blink or move, the giants will come back for sure," his great-grandmother Nubar assured him.

He would gather as much air as he could into his lungs, put his palm to his chest, and count, soundlessly moving his lips, breathing out slowly, trying not to blink or move. Each time he failed, he felt pangs of guilt: he couldn't achieve his goal; he was unable to do it. It seemed to him that somewhere there, behind the horizon, the giants stood shoulder to shoulder, somber and forgotten by everyone, smoking their long *chibukhs* and waiting for the hour when one of the children would finally manage to hold still at the mouth of the cave for three hundred heartbeats. He was convinced that behind the line of the distant mountains he could see the tips of the giants' felt peasant hats poking the skies. The smoke of their long pipes fashioned from pear trees gathered into humid clouds, which then rained for a long time, turning the wheat fields into an impassable swamp. The north wind got tangled in their giant beards, and every time they started combing their beards out, the wind would escape, bringing with it a long and cold winter. That is what his great-grandmother Nubar used to tell him before he fell asleep.

"How I loved her stories!" sighs Mishik, going around the foot of Giants' Cliff. The last time he saw the cave was when he took his son and daughter for a visit. Satenik was eight years old then, Mamikon six. Mishik took them around the cave, showed them all the hidden corners, and retold great-grandmother Nubar's *azhdahak* stories. His children listened, spellbound. Satenik seemed to have stopped breathing; she stared at him with wide-opened eyes and only timidly smiled. Mamikon was sniffling and sighing. And then, out of nowhere, he said, "I want some tea!"

"Where would I get tea for you in a cave?" Mishik marveled. His son looked disheartened.

"It smells like sweet tea."

Mishik could not bring himself to admit that he also smelled tea. Stupidly, he felt embarrassed: What would his children think about him? Later, he reproached himself many times for this foolish indecisiveness: his son certainly would have been pleased to know that he was not the only one to smell sweet thyme tea in the cave.

That day they stayed until evening, dangling their legs over the abyss and looking out for the tips of giants' hats behind the ridge of the snowy mountain pass.

"Can you see them?" Mishik asked.

"We can," the children responded with conviction, and he had no doubt that they meant it.

WHEN AVAKANTS MISHIK REACHES the old *khachkar*, he starts by greeting it: "Hello, *khachkar-jan*, how are you doing so far away from us?" He unwraps his offerings and leaves them amid the roots of an old oak tree growing nearby, each time explaining in great detail: "The coffee is for Marina; she can't do without it. The dried fruit is also for her. But the candy," he stumbles over the words burning the roof of his mouth, but then, calming down, continues, "is for Mamikon." He takes off his suit jacket and spreads it out on the left side of the *khachkar*, close to the heart of stone. He sits there for a long time, leaning against its cold shoulder. He shares with it the recent news.

Satenik will have to take her exams soon; she is studying to be a doctor. It's hard, but she likes it. She has found a fiancé, a nice guy, smart, but from the village of Movses. It is right on the border. There is shooting every day, but what can you do? Nowadays there is shooting everywhere.

Having shared all the news, Mishik falls silent. He tries not to disturb the evening felicity with sad ruminations, but he inevitably returns to the day when he lost his wife and son. He remembers how Mamikon was playing in the yard when the shelling started. How Marina raced outside to take their son into the cellar. How right then a projectile hit their yard. How they were buried in the same coffin, whatever could be recovered of the two of them collected into a meager heap. How Satenik did not sleep after that for many days, and how one day she put on her mother's best outfit—a light chiffon dress, graceful leather open-toe shoes with high heels, gold jewelry—and went strolling through Berd. She walked like a tightrope walker, her hands held out on either side—otherwise, she wouldn't have been able to stay balanced on those heels. She was walking and smiling.

Mishik begins heading home when a chilly evening blueness comes over the sky. He departs with a parting bow to the *khachkar* and to the old oak tree.

"I am grateful that I still have my daughter, because otherwise what would be the point of living?" he says without thinking who exactly his interlocutor is. He expresses his gratitude every time he rounds the foot of Giants' Cliff. The sky, condensing rapidly, closes its cool palms over the canyon. The stars twinkle, each a broken heart.

Great-grandmother Nubar used to say that there is so much unspent love in broken human hearts that God, when their time comes, lifts them up into heaven and they disperse the inconsolable inky darkness with their glow. Satenik often repeats that one day her father's heart will also shine upon the world. "There is so much love in you, Daddy, there is so much unspent love in your broken heart!"

In response he only shrugs his shoulders and clears his throat in embarrassment—"What are you saying, daughter?"

"I know what I am talking about," insists Satenik.

By the time Avakants Mishik reaches the foot of Giants' Cliff, the ever-present crows have whisked off his offerings to their nests. On the cool side of the *khachkar*, leaving behind a wet trace, crawls a vine snail, carrying the whole world on its back. The old oak tree sheds its first leaves tinted with autumn red, the first frosts fall at night, October is right around the corner. On the threshold of the cave, dangling their feet in leather *trekhs* over the abyss and shifting to the back of their heads their sharp-tipped hats, sit the invisible *azhdahaks*. Their long pipes are smoking, the sweet thyme tea is growing cold, but they don't touch it. They follow Avakants Mishik with their mournful eyes and wipe away their enormous giants' tears.

Thunderstorm

—————

Grandma Siran insists that Yepimeh has a light bulb burning inside her, because her face always beams with a smile, even when she's asleep.

One cannot argue with Grandma Siran; she knows her own granddaughter better than anyone. Any event is a source of joy for Yepimeh: it rains, and she is happy; frosts in May, so what? "The weather is also entitled to mood swings," smiles Yepimeh and looks on as only she can—with eyes wide open, with her whole heart, with her whole soul.

Patients really like her. One can always hear in the hall of the surgery floor: "Yepimeh-jan, where are you? Come on over, we have something to tell you."

She puts away the mop, gathers her loose hair under her snow-white kerchief. She rinses her hands, straightens the seam of her robe. When she stops by a hospital room, she lights it up with her smile.

"Here, Yepimeh-jan," the patients offer her different treats.

She accepts only a single thing from each person: a cookie, an apple, a tangerine. She leaves, carefully pressing the treats to her chest.

Old Ambo has a broken ankle: for some reason he climbed up to the attic and, unlike all normal people, decided to walk over the roof. And lo and behold, the roof tiles gave way under his weight. He tumbled down ten feet and nearly killed himself. He screamed himself hoarse, but who would hear him? After all, his house is on the very edge of Berd; all there is on the other side is the river, the old chapel, and the wheat field, fringed at the far end by the forest. It's a good thing Grandma Siran suspected something was wrong: she hadn't seen Ambo pass by her gate for some time, eyesore that he was. She stopped by his house, and there he was, lying amid the broken tile, angry as a wasp, and cussing Providence to high heaven.

They put him in a shared hospital room but then had to transfer him to a private room: he made too much fuss and kept everyone up. He grumbled, groaned, found choice words for his cast, complained now about the heat, now about the cold, cursed the day and the hour when he decided to clean up the attic. It had been filled with junk for a hundred years; it could have stayed as it was.

"Was it so hard to ask Yepimeh to help you with the cleaning?" Grandma Siran grumbled as the ambulance made its way to the hospital, jumping over the potholes created the previous spring when the river flooded and destroyed the road. Ambo did not deign to answer; he did not so much as turn his head toward her. After all, she was the one who had abandoned him, so she could stop pretending that she cared! But when she took him by his hand, he did not yank it away, only frowned so that she would not get too comfortable. But Siran was not one to relax: she consulted in detail with the doctor, and the very next day packed up and left for the city to get him crutches. Ambo was scheduled to be discharged in a week, and he would still be wearing a cast at home. He would have to relearn how to walk little by little.

Yepimeh stops by old Ambo's hospital room right after lunch, when the patients, having taken their prescribed pills, are about to settle down for their afternoon nap. She spreads the treats on the bedside table: a cookie, a tangerine, an apple. She pulls up a chair and folds her hands on her knees. She smiles.

Old Ambo knows what follows; that is why he sighs loudly and grudgingly. Yepimeh ignores it.

"Tell me," she implores him, combing out her grandfather's messy beard.

"What is there to tell? My foot hurts, my head feels like it is pressed inside an iron hoop, my blood pressure is at it again, they keep forcing these pills on me, but I am not one to listen to them! My cast hurts and itches, I wish I could scratch my skin off with my nails, but I can't reach that far!"

Yepimeh tinkers with his fingers.

"Tell me!"

"My insomnia knows no mercy, the worms have spoiled the hazelnuts, I have to save the trees before it's too late. The sun is biting, burning me as if through a magnifying glass, which means there will be a thunderstorm this evening. And the crow crows as if insulted, which means the weather will get worse, and the thunderstorm will bring cold air."

"Tell me!"

"You're starting again?"

Yepimeh peels the tangerine, hands it to him. Old Ambo eats one slice and hands the next one to her. That is how they eat tangerines: he has one slice, she gets the other. They break the cookie in half as well, but Ambo refuses the apple: he doesn't like them. Yepimeh rolls it on her palm, then tucks it into her pocket.

"Tell me!"

Old Ambo raises his eyes toward the ceiling and sighs deeply. "That stubbornness of yours, who did you get it from?"

"From you."

"Ahem, fine. So here it is. Twenty years ago, on the snowiest day of the year—I don't know why, but in Berd, so much snow falls on the second of February that it takes half a day to clear a path to the gate, and then by the evening, after the snow is over, the frost hits so hard that you have to keep adding firewood to the stove all night or you'll freeze to death . . . What was I talking about?" Ambo stops.

"Twenty years ago . . ." Yepimeh reminds him in a whisper.

He hastily picks up again. "You were born on February second. But joy and sorrow go hand in hand everywhere: the moment we rejoiced about your birth, your mother, deciding that she had lived enough, became an angel and flew to the heavens."

"An angel with wings?" clarifies Yepimeh.

"What? Ah yes, with wings. And Grandma Siran brought you up herself. You were sick a lot when you were little, oh boy, did you get sick a lot! The slightest draft and you'd go down with fever and cough for at least a week, if not two."

Old Ambo frowns, pained by his memories or perhaps by his injured ankle.

"They told us all kinds of things: that you were too weak, that you wouldn't make it. That we needed to put you into a special boarding school, where other kids like you lived. But your grandma and I wouldn't give in . . ."

"Is that because you are stubborn like me?"

"Yes, because we are stubborn like you. We didn't give you to anybody, we kept you for ourselves. And little by little you came around, learned how to speak and even read and write. You completed eight grades at school. And now that you are old enough, you are helping in the hospital. I cannot even imagine what they would do without your help!"

Yepimeh lies down next to her grandfather and rests her head on his shoulder. He kisses her fluffy hair. Vahan had the same hair: light, almost weightless, not Armenian-looking at all. Siran saved a lock of his baby hair as a keepsake; she was convinced that his hair would get darker when he grew up. Vahan's hair became thicker with age, but it never lost its unusual golden tint. He could be spotted easily in any group of kids because he gleamed like the sun. He was their only and much-awaited child, their souls' joy and consolation. He married early, right after school: he wanted to make sure that his mother and father got a chance to enjoy their grandkids. He left to serve in the army. The war came a month later. When the enemy surrounded him, he refused to surrender and blew himself up with a grenade. The daughter-in-law died in childbirth. Yepimeh was born not like other children. She would never get married or continue their line. The Didevants clan ended with her.

Siran left him right after they buried their daughter-in-law. She stayed in bed, her eyes dry, for three days and then begged him: please let me go. If I stay, I will go mad with grief and drive you mad too. He let her go.

They live on the opposite ends of the same street. He lives in his house; she and the granddaughter live in theirs.

On the weekends Yepimeh always comes to visit her grandfather. She brings him dinner that her grandmother has made and adds the treats that she gets from the hospital patients. The grandpa eats the grandma's cooking as if doing her a favor.

"She never learned how to properly salt the food," he grumbles, scraping his plate clean with a spoon.

He sends his pension to Siran with his granddaughter, everything to the last penny. When he passes by his former wife's house, he never turns his head. Siran watches him through the curtains, shakes her head, and remains silent.

Didevants Ambo is lying in the hospital bed, hugging his granddaughter, his nose buried in her hair. Life is not endless: he and Siran will go, leaving Yepimeh behind. Then his daughter-in-law's brother Aleksan will look after her. He is a kind and gentle man, otherwise they would have never entrusted their granddaughter to him.

Didevants Yepimeh is curled up against her grandfather's shoulder. She thinks that he is probably God because everything in the world happens exactly as he predicts: if tomorrow is your birthday, then there will be so much snow that you'll spend half the day clearing a path all the way to the gate, and at night you'll go to the stove several times to feed it more firewood. And if the sun does not warm but instead bites as if burning through a magnifying glass, then he says there will be a thunderstorm in the evening. And the thunderstorm always comes.

Hunger

Nemetsants Aleksan lingers in the cellar to feast his eyes on the fruits of his daily labor: the broad-necked clay pots, whose aromas give away their contents even with the lids closed: this one has pickled cabbage, the ones over there have marinated beets, chervil, and purslane, all nestled up next to homemade cheese of every variety—fatty *brynza*, mildly brined *chanakh*, stringy *chechil*, ripe sheep's milk cheese with herbs. Through the dark glass of their potbellied jars, honey and clarified butter emit an incandescent glow. The big storage bin is tightly packed with bags small and large containing various sorts of flour, dried fruit, nuts, and grain; the smaller bin, with peas, beans, and wheat. The ceiling is hung with smoked meats: ham dressed in a thin layer of fat, links of homemade sausage, fiery-hot pork belly roulade trussed snugly with twine. The shelves are crowded with jars of winter preserves: fruit jams and jellies, compotes, stewed meat, baked and stewed vegetables. The potato pit is filled to the brim with choice tubers layered with dried river sand; carrots, beets, and cabbage lie packed in wooden boxes with ventilation holes to keep the vegetables fresh. Clusters of grapes and ears of dried corn hang from the sturdy beams; apples and pears sit waiting for their designated hour; persimmons, sun-colored and sweet, are slowly ripening; quinces glisten buttery-yellow underneath their delicate fuzz. Watermelons, lined up in a row, rest against the wall with their striped sides, daydreaming of summer.

Nemetsants Aleksan and his wife, Arpenik, have a big farmstead: two orchards, a vegetable garden, a chicken coop, an apiary thirty beehives strong, a rabbit hutch, a barn big enough to house three cows and eight sheep, and a pigpen. While Aleksan is out breaking his back over the harvest, his wife takes care of the house and the animals: she does all the washing, cleaning, and feeding, and takes the cattle out to pasture. From dawn till dusk, she bustles about in the kitchen, baking, frying, sautéing, boiling. Making winter preserves is painstakingly hard; *ghaurma* alone takes so much effort—first, the meat has to be braised with spices over low heat for almost twenty-four hours (to the point of fainting, Arpenik likes to joke), then it has to be packed into jars with scalding hot butter and canned immediately before it cools. The canned meat goes a long way in the lean winter months—just fry it up with eggs or add it to any soup or porridge. Aleksan lends his wife a hand whenever he can steal a moment from his own work: he'll fire-roast the eggplant-tomatoes-peppers here, purée the raspberries with sugar for jam there, or grind the roasted wheat into *pokhindz*[1] in the stone mill—Arpenik doesn't trust the new electric grinders and prefers to use the old intractable contraption she has inherited from her great-grandmother. Arpenik is reluctant to accept her husband's help and keeps trying to convince him to take a quick nap instead—get some sleep and give your arm a little rest. He obliges, but after tossing and turning for a few minutes, comes back to her. She shakes her

---

1 A coarse flour used for porridge (*khavits*) in the winter.

head disapprovingly but doesn't say anything. What *can* she say—at their age, insomnia is the norm.

They send some of what they make to their adoptive daughter, leave a small portion for themselves, and sell most of it at the farmers' market where the townsfolk go to stock up on market days. Aleksan is unfailingly polite and patient with them; townsfolk are like kids—they know nothing about fruits and vegetables and can't even tell *salceson*[2] from ham. He explains, in detail, which apples to buy for now and which for storing, expounds on how and with what to eat the cured meats, offering samples that he cuts not in little translucent slices but in generous big pieces. Some of the customers gratefully accept his advice, others politely cut him off—thanks, we'll figure it out. He never insists—my job is to explain, the rest is up to you. Some of the customers are so unpleasant that he wonders how the earth carries them—condescending and rude, they buy from him as if doing him a favor. He treats the fact of their existence with resignation: say what you will, every herd has a bad sheep. What good would it do to get worked up over something you can't change?

ASK ALEKSAN what his biggest fear is, and he'll answer without hesitation: hunger. Pain can be soothed with medicine, cold can be spooked off with warmth, fear can be chatted away. But nothing can placate or cheat hunger; it hovers overhead in a cloud of infernal darkness, taunting you and killing every shred of your humanity. Aleksan is intimately acquainted with hunger; he lived with it for two endlessly long years, for twenty-five terrifying months: the winter when, never imagining that Berd would soon be under siege, people carelessly cleaned out their winter preserves and found themselves with

2 A dry sausage, from the French *saucisson*.

nothing to eat in February; the spring when they were bombed
during peak sowing season, preventing people from working
in the fields; the summer when the entire sky was blanketed
by smoke from the torched wheat fields; the fall when they
couldn't even make it to the forest to forage for wild fruits; the
winter when a tiny trickle of aid—grain, powdered milk and
eggs, and tea—finally started getting through the mountain
pass that was under constant enemy shelling, so that at least the
kids could hold out until the arrival of warmer weather, while
the grownups, and especially the elderly, departed one after the
other; you'd wake up in the morning to find Grandma dead
already, and Grandpa would be barely breathing and gone by
sunset; the following spring when, desperate enough to ignore
the enemy fire, the people went out into the fields to till, and
not everybody came back—some were cut down by bullets,
others taken hostage, but there was no other alternative: war or
hunger, it was all the same death; the summer when hail the
size of human fists destroyed everything, literally everything,
except the potatoes, which the people hoped would last them
till spring; the fall when the harvest began disappearing from
fields and orchards, and they all suspected each other at first
until they discovered that it was the townspeople; it turned
out they were starving too, but didn't know how to live off the
land, so they were stealing from the villagers. Aleksan found
this upsetting but he couldn't help pitying the townsfolk: How
could you hold a grudge against people who had been driven by
despair over the treacherous mountain pass to scavenge food for
their families by theft?

"Nothing can be more frightening than hunger," thought
Aleksan, and he knew exactly what he was saying because he
had stared hunger straight in the face. It had come to him
in the guise of an emaciated old man with sunken cheeks,

a thread-thin line of bloodless lips, and papery skin stretched taut over his sharply protruding cheekbones. "If you weren't careful, you could cut yourself running your finger over them," randomly flashed through Aleksan's mind. It was as if the old man could sense his thoughts; his translucent eyelids, under which a slight movement of his dark pupils was detectable, flickered, but he couldn't muster the strength to open them. He was lying on his side, his neck awkwardly twisted and his left arm splayed on the other side, his chin pointing up, and faint traces left by dried tears ran from the outer corners of his eyes toward his temples; in a senselessly repetitive motion, he kept clawing at handfuls of frozen soil with his right hand; his pants had slid down, revealing his sunken stomach and the flabby funnel of his belly button; his leg had turned black and was bleeding where the trap had snapped around it, crushing the bone to a pulp. He was silent the entire way as Aleksan drove him to the hospital, and only grimaced slightly when the car hit potholes. As he was being moved to a gurney, he clutched Aleksan's hand and pulled him down. Aleksan, leaning over to make out the words through the old man's raspy, labored breathing, went pale, and then mouthed: "Just give me the address, I will handle the rest." The old man mustered the strength to tell him the address.

From the hospital, Aleksan headed straight to Musheghants Tsolak's house. Tsolak was out back, chopping wood. When he saw his guest, he set down the axe and went to greet him, ready with a smile and a handshake. Aleksan made a tight fist and punched him once, then a second time, right in his smiling lips. Dodging a return blow, he ducked and, without taking his eyes off Tsolak's face, felt for a log. Wincing from the pain that shot through his crippled left arm, Aleksan clobbered Tsolak in the stomach with all his might. Tsolak went down with a sob. Aleksan stood over him for a bit, waiting for his rage to subside, then spat and rubbed his saliva into the ground with his boot. Then he plopped down and helped Tsolak turn over onto his back.

"Why did you set a bear trap on your plot?" demanded Aleksan, still short of breath and stuttering, "What were you hoping to catch? A jackal?"

"What trap?"

"Don't play dumb," Aleksan spat out angrily.

"Who got caught in the trap?"

"An old man. A refugee."

"So, if he is a refugee, then it's fine for him to steal?" Tsolak sat up, swung around with unexpected adroitness, and slapped Aleksan across the face. Aleksan neither dodged the blow nor tried to return it. He swallowed, noting the unpleasant taste of his own blood.

"He's definitely going to lose his leg. That's if he pulls through. He has a great-granddaughter in town and nobody else. He lost everyone else in the pogroms."

Tsolak got up, picked up the log that Aleksan had used to clobber him, and tossed it back into the mound of chopped firewood without looking. The log landed at the very top, got caught on another log by a chipped piece of bark, and hung suspended in the air.

"So, my kids aren't kids, then?" he hissed in a whisper. "Half of my relatives are not refugees, right? It's OK to steal from me, right? Because I'm a pansy and not a man, right? And I don't have a right to eat?"

Aleksan also got up and dusted off his pants.

"Anyway, I'm off. You are in charge of the old man."

"Off where?"

"To get his great-granddaughter from town. He says she hasn't eaten for five days."

It was a long ride to town, four hours over a road torn and gutted by shelling. The town struck Aleksan as oppressive; it looked exactly like the border villages—just as deserted, forlorn, and steeped in gloomy darkness and cold. Every house, every street, every window exuded desperation and loneliness. He had no trouble finding the old man's apartment in a dank neighborhood on the outskirts of the city, on the first floor of a ten-story cement construction, whose windows, down to the last one, were hung with blankets on the inside in a desperate effort to preserve whatever scant warmth there was. The girl's eyes, as it turned out, were of two different colors: one green, the other hazel. Aleksan's great-grandmother would have called it the devil's mark, which he left sometimes so that people wouldn't forget about his presence. Aleksan offered the girl a handful of dried prunes, which she accepted after some hesitation, and not before thanking him. She ate slowly, with dignity. When she was finished, Aleksan told her to pack all of their belongings, hers and her great-grandfather's, and she complied without complaining or asking questions. They made it back to Berd around midnight. They raced through the mountain pass so fast they risked missing a turn or plummeting off a cliff, but there was no other way—car headlights make excellent targets for sharpshooters. Mercifully, they made it home without incident.

The old man passed away that very same night—his heart couldn't take it. Aleksan buried him next to his own parents. The girl cried all the time, didn't answer any of their questions, was afraid of darkness and closed doors, and screamed if someone shut the door to her room. It took a while for Aleksan

to figure out what it was she feared, but it finally occurred to
him to take the door off its hinges, and she calmed down at
once. Her name was Anna, and she was twelve, although she
looked barely nine: small, frail, quiet. She ate very little, tried
not to leave the house if she could avoid it, and if she went
outside, she didn't go past the yard. Once, she wrapped her
arms around Aleksan and told him, in a terrifying whisper,
that once upon a time everything used to be wonderful in
her life, that both of her grandparents were schoolteachers in
Baku, that her father built houses while her mother raised her
younger brother, but how one day they were all gone because
some people stormed into their apartment and killed everyone
except Anna—at the last moment, her grandmother had
shoved her underneath the sofa and told her to stay put no
matter what, but she didn't have time to also hide her four-
year-old grandson, and Anna saw how someone's dirty boot
tripped him as he was trying to run away, how he fell, banged
his face against the floor, and started crying, and how the same
dirty boots landed full force on his back, jumping on it until
the boy stopped moving. Her great-grandfather smuggled
Anna out of Baku in a suitcase—he made holes in the sides to
make sure she didn't suffocate before making his way through
the pogrom-engulfed city. Before shutting the suitcase lid, he
asked for her forgiveness in case they both got killed.

"But we didn't get killed, as you can see," she concluded,
raising her wondrous varicolored eyes to Aleksan. "Please
don't be mad at him, he used to be a scientist and didn't
know anything other than his science. When we got here, he
found a job as a night guard, but they were holding back his
pay. Nobody would lend us money because we were refugees.
We had to make rent for the room because the landlady kept
threatening to kick us out, I kept crying all the time because I

really wanted to eat, and my great-grandpa put up with it for as long as he could. Then he said he couldn't stand to see my tears and went to find us some food."

ASK ALEKSAN what the purpose of human life is, and he'll say without hesitation: caring for others. For relatives, for loved ones, for all the ones who remain. Of all his kids, only the youngest survived the war. Now he lives in faraway America and only visits once in a while. He keeps asking his parents to come live with him, but they won't budge—the graves of our forebears are here, and this is where we will lie as well. Anna has long moved to the big city and become a journalist; now she travels all over the world writing clever articles. Everyone seems to have found a place in life, so Aleksan and his wife can finally breathe a sigh of relief and live for themselves. But there is also Yepimeh, the sunshine girl, the daughter of Aleksan's sister who died in childbirth. Aleksan and Arpenik visit her every Sunday, both to see how she's doing and to remind her of them—she's got a birdlike memory and only recognizes people whom she sees regularly. When the time comes, they will have her come live with them. Life has meaning for as long as you have someone to take care of, Aleksan likes to say. Arpenik doesn't disagree—what's the point of arguing if he is completely right: life only has meaning if you have someone to live for.

Lace

Derbent[1] resembled a faded copper incuse set in a simple wooden frame: trees with branches caught in the hem of the sky and burned by the breath of the sun; stone houses with high glassed-in porches, dusty knots of back alleys, a red citadel with an infinite number of steps leading up to it. Anna tried to count them as she climbed up but soon gave up: What did it matter how many there were? She stopped midway to catch her breath and to take in the oriental city, beautiful in its reticence. Out of the corner of her eye she caught a glimpse of the sharp dome of the Armenian Apostolic church and sighed with a mixed feeling of contentment and bitterness: no place is complete without us! On that day, she found herself in Derbent for the first time and wasn't familiar with the city at all, but she was not apprehensive; there was something fleetingly, unconditionally, and immediately familiar about it. This familiar feeling was probably inspired by the loud courtyards surrounded by the low picket fences, or perhaps by the faces of the passersby: in each of them she recognized one of her Berd neighbors. Or perhaps it was the mellifluous chorus of voices that spoke a language that did not grate against her ear because it sounded so similar to

---

1 A city in the Republic of Dagestan, Russia, located on the Caspian Sea.

Armenian. Anna had spent only a couple of hours in Derbent, but she already managed to identify in it some features of Berd, which she always sought when visiting any city, and which she unfailingly found. It didn't matter where she was: in sun-singed Spain, in mysterious and incomprehensible China, or in windblown Scandinavia. Everywhere, in every place there was a message waiting for her from the town that had become her own; it made itself known in the red-colored roof tiles, in the worn-out thresholds of the stone house, or in the aroma of a toasty slice of sourdough bread. I am here, I am nearby, her town called to her, you have a place to which you can return, you have a haven where you will never be afraid to live!

It had been fourteen years since Anna started relearning how not to be afraid to live. Since the day Aleksan materialized in the doorway and handed her a fistful of dried fruit: "Eat slowly, otherwise you'll get a bellyache." As she accepted the precious treat, she remembered that she had to leave some for her great-grandpa, and she was chewing deliberately slowly so that she could trick hunger and feel full before the dried fruit ran out. But the fruit ran out before she felt full.

Far away, in its turquoise-blue shimmer, the handsome Caspian Sea was lazily sorting its waves. Anna remembered the sea since the days of her pre-pogrom childhood, which she had erased from her life irrevocably and forever. But the sea appeared in her dreams, uninvited and always catching her unawares; it ruthlessly scorched her soul, leaving behind the feeling of irredeemable bitterness and loss. Most often, she dreamed of the sea promenade, where the whole family liked to go for walks. "Let's go for a walk," her mother would suggest, and everyone agreed; Mom was the loudest of everybody, her laughter was boisterous and unrestrained, her head thrown back, her body doubled over, her arms flailing. Anna loved it, and she often mimicked her mother's gestures and facial expressions; her father pushed the stroller Gosha was sleeping in—they had waited so long for him, and here he was; the chestnut trees were in bloom, the Caspian was reflecting the sky and seemed to be its extension; Anna was laughing, flailing her arms like her mother, and she knew that things would always be this way. These happy and bright dreams would turn into a trying ordeal for her on awakening: she had to live for some time with the feeling of tightness in her heart, as if someone squeezed it with clawed paws just enough to allow it to beat without letting go.

The midday was blinding her with annoying sunshine, sparrows were chirping, and near the very foot of the citadel, young people were sharing a funny story, interrupting each other with uproarious laughter.

Anna shook herself from her thoughts. Scolding herself yet again for dwelling on the painful memories, which she never learned to ward off, she resumed her climb. She had to hurry: she still had, on her itinerary for the day, the visit to Kyrkhlyar, a necropolis where, according to legend, rested forty Arab martyrs who prevailed in battle against a forty-thousand-strong army of Khazars. Despite her generally intolerant attitude toward any warriors of faith, Anna wanted to visit the cemetery, which the locals considered a sacred source of pride.

It was already long past midday when she finally made it to the necropolis. The sun had crossed the summit of the sky, and, reducing its meager warmth, was resignedly rolling toward sunset; the air over the city grew dense as if it had grown heavier; a flock of seagulls circled over the Caspian with hoarse, anguished cries. By the cemetery entrance, on a narrow wooden bench, sat an ancient woman in a black full-coverage dress and worn shoes, her hands raised in prayer and her lips moving wordlessly. Anna wanted to pass by, but noticed her look, detached and unseeing, and stopped, holding her breath in admiration.

The old woman was distinguished, with the kind of noble beauty that open, kindhearted people acquire in the autumn of their years: deep wrinkles did not disfigure but rather beautified her face; her hands, covered in reddish age spots, resembled two clay saucers in which one serves honey and butter for breakfast; there was so much unassuming and unconditional dignity in her appearance that even her worn shoes did not spoil that beauty but rather emphasized and complemented it.

Having finished her prayer, the old woman moved aside, making space on the bench and said, patting it with the palm of her hand: "*Kyzym, otur ianmida.*"

Anna shrank inside as she heard Azerbaijani words, and then she looked behind her, hoping that they were addressed to someone else. But there was nobody else around.

"Take a seat here, daughter," the old woman repeated, this time in Russian.

Anna sat down. Contrary to her expectations, the old woman was not in a hurry to strike up a conversation. With the palm of her hand she stroked her chest, as if brushing away invisible dust particles, and then sighed deeply. She wove her fingers into a whimsical knot, and Anna involuntarily smiled at this long-forgotten gesture from her childhood.

"How could you tell that I was a woman?" she asked, trying to break the silence and then immediately regretted it: after all, it was impolite to remind people of their handicap. But the old woman shrugged her shoulders, unperturbed, not finding anything objectionable in her words.

"Women breathe deeper and slower," she explained. "Men don't breathe, they just play around. That is their attitude toward life as well: they do not live it, they burn it."

Anna nodded in agreement but immediately checked herself: after all, her interlocutor could not see her nodding and might consider her silence rude. But before she opened her mouth to respond, the old lady continued:

"You're not from around here. Are you visiting for fun or for work?"

"There's going to be a big festival tomorrow, as you probably know. I'll be reporting on it. I just came a little early so I could see Derbent. I won't have any time afterward."

The old woman straightened out the hem of her dress, smoothed it out over her knees, and craned her neck, as if trying to see someone.

"Do you see a white car? It's time for my grandson to come pick me up."

"I don't see it. But I can take you home. Just give me the address, and I will get you a cab."

"Thank you, daughter, there is no need for that; my grandson will come get me. He brings me here every day and then picks me up. I can only pray here. I can't do it at home: there's too much noise and bustle. Here, it's so quiet I can even hear the wind breathing."

"You put it so nicely: the wind breathing."

The old lady chuckled bitterly: "I read it in some book, I can't remember the name now. We used to have a huge library. I used to read a lot when my eyes could see. But I went blind thirty years ago, so I no longer read."

Anna caught herself thinking that she really wanted to touch the old lady. She even reached for her but pulled her hand back. The old lady turned her head slightly, as if listening to her movements, grew silent looking in front of her with her blind eyes, and clucked her tongue.

"Is there something you want to ask me?"

"There is," Anna replied eagerly. "You said that you lost your eyesight years ago. If you don't mind and if my question isn't insulting to you, could you tell me—what are your most vivid memories? The memories that you remember in snapshots."

The old lady sighed.

"There are things that never get erased from memory: faces of parents and children, the paternal house, the evening sunset over the Caspian and the street leading to the marketplace; I spent my entire childhood skipping up and down that street because my father was a vegetable vendor and used to send me on little chores everywhere. I remember the old mosque with a big stork's nest on its minaret. Every time the muezzin called the people to prayer, the stork would fly up to the edge of its nest and freeze at attention for the entire duration of the service, as if standing guard. One time it flew south and did not come back; everybody thought it had perished during the journey, but it finally did return by July. It was weak and sick; it collapsed on the threshold of the mosque and expired. I see it even now, the mullah carrying the stork his arms like some priceless cargo, like a fragile glass vessel, with tears of pure, sincere sorrow streaming down his face."

She fell silent, as if unsure whether to continue, and then resumed, but not before finding Anna's hand and covering it with her light palm.

"I also remember the lace: silky, weightless, like dandelion fluff. I have never seen anything more beautiful in my life. I was only five back then, perhaps even younger. I woke up from some unclear noise, and, groggy, couldn't distinguish at first where it was coming from; then I understood that it was coming from the outside. I rushed out into the yard exactly as I was and peeked outside the gate: there was a whole crowd of half-dressed people walking down our street, old women with their shawls hastily thrown over their shoulders, men in their undergarments, women in their nightgowns, children in their pajamas. Armed men were driving them out from the middle part of town, where rich Armenian and Jewish merchants lived. The morning was chilly and overcast; they hadn't been given a chance to dress and were shivering from the cold, helplessly pulling their scant clothing around themselves to warm up a little. Those who hadn't managed to put on shoes limped along on tender feet. The adults, despite their desperate state—they definitely knew how this was going to end—were walking in silence, their eyes fixed on the ground beneath their feet; the children would periodically start to whine but would immediately fall quiet. Raising their palms skyward, the old women were praying and begging for salvation, and their sorrowful complaints were more frightening than anything else in this most frightening reality. One of them, just as she passed me, put her hand inside her bosom and pulled out a small baptismal cross, kissed it three times and squeezed it with such confidence, as if this could have changed anything. I, impatiently jumping up and down in the opening of the gate, was waiting until she passed because I had noticed behind her two girls in similar dresses: high bodices, sleeves decorated with the most elaborate stitch, puffy skirts barely reaching their knees and hemmed across the bottom with lace, the likes of which I, a child from a poor family, had only heard about but never seen. That lace, light and transparent, trembled and fell again as it was picked up by the icy wind's breath, like the wings of overthrown angels, like the feathers of rare birds, like the pure tidal sea foam. When the girls

drew abreast of me, I, growing bold, stretched out my hands
and touched the hems of their dresses. The lace was the color
of milk foam, light and weightless, embroidered with silver
irises and some petals which I did not have time to make out.
No words can convey the state of ineffable and profound grief
that befell me at that moment, when I precociously realized
that the beauty of this lace had nothing to do with me! The
lace was like the curls left by frost on the frozen windows of a
shushaband; you can't have enough of them, but they will never
belong to you. That is what I experienced at that moment,
the feeling of inconsolable loss that overwhelms anyone who
momentarily catches a glimpse of the world of magic only to
get shut out once and for all. Disarmed by the revelation, I
walked, as if in a trance, between the two girls, not letting
go the hems of their dresses. They did not act surprised or try
to pry me off; they only looked at me with their bottomless
eyes, their faces pale. Their lips went purple from the cold. The
smaller of the two had eyes of two different colors: one was
green and the other was brown; my mother would say that it
is the sign of Iblis:[2] sometimes he marks people as a reminder
of his presence in human life. I would have kept walking that
way between the girls, but suddenly one of the men behind
us grabbed me and shoved me inside a random gate. Before
I had a chance to cry from fear and insult, he shouted: 'Stay
there, or you'll be mistaken for one of us!' He probably saved
my life, that man, for I had run out of the house half dressed,
and I would have been pushed ahead along with everybody.
And I would have encountered the same fate as that entire
crowd of doomed people: they would have shot me and

2 Iblis or al-Shaytān is a figure frequently recurring in the Quran, sometimes
identified as a jinn and sometimes as an angel who fell from grace. Iblis holds an
ambivalent role in Islamic traditions.

thrown me in the Caspian for fish food. There were people, and—poof!—they were gone, vanished like chimney smoke in the cold November air."

Anna gasped. The old woman's palm that was covering her hand felt like a block of stone that flattened and pressed her to the ground.

"Afterward, the inhabitants of Derbent plundered those people's property," the old lady continued after a momentary silence, "but my father brought back nothing but a cart of books, which was the only thing that he didn't consider stealing. We grew up on those books, my three sisters, five brothers, and me, a big and close-knit family, the pride of our city; ask anyone about Asiyat Mamedova and her family, and you won't hear a single bad word about us."

"You guessed that I am Armenian," Anna whispered.

The old lady stroked her hand.

"It is what it is, daughter."

Anna did not visit Kyrkhlyar that day. She sat with the old woman until her grandson came to pick her up. She watched as he reverentially led his grandmother to the car, how he carefully put her in the seat and wrapped her feet with a blanket. Anna refused his offer to take her to the hotel. When the car started moving, the old lady turned her head toward Anna and made an odd gesture with her hand, as if pressing down something heavy. Anna felt how the imaginary vise that was squeezing her temples weakened its grip, but she wasn't sure whether what she felt was pain or relief. When she saw a segment from Baku on the evening news, for the first time she did not change the channel and just watched silently how the head of state, surrounded by foreign guests, laid wreaths in the Alley of Martyrs, the place of the city's mourning. In that alley lay buried the perpetrators of the Armenian pogroms who were

shot by Soviet soldiers. The government of the country, trying
to white out the nation's shameful past, had promoted them
to the rank of warriors of faith. Anna peered into the gloomy
faces of men etched on the tombstones and tried to guess which
one of them had worn those boots that jumped on her brother's
back. She also thought how Gosha, although still a mere child
who didn't understand much, had seen how their grandma
had pushed her under the sofa; he could have darted over there
for cover as well when strangers burst into the house; after all,
that's what he always did—run to Anna and hide behind her
back when scared. But he didn't that day; that day he ran past
her because he did not want to reveal her hiding place to the
men who had come to murder them.

Herd

The November morning, diligent housekeeper that it was, bustled around making sure everything was in perfect order. After blowing out the stars and giving the sky one last wipe with a clean wet cloth, having made sure, with a deep sense of satisfaction, that everything upstairs was ready to greet the rising sun, the morning applied itself to the valley: it smoothed the treetops ruffled by the night winds, awakened the mountain rivers, and generously sprinkled dew over the raised road dust. The November morning, cool and clear, busily tidied up, preparing the world for a balmy, pleasant day. Right around the time the morning cast one final satisfied look over the beauty it had created and settled down underneath the stone wall of the church to take a quick nap before sunrise, Kapitonants Manush opened her eyes. She hurriedly said a quick prayer and chugged down a glass of mint-infused water on an empty stomach to ward off the foul mood and bile that, she firmly believed, accumulated over-night in her innards so that it could eat them from the inside with renewed zeal come the new day. Then she tied a cotton kerchief over her hair, wrapped her shoulders in a plaid woolen shawl (squares of dark blue over pale), and headed for the door, exercising utmost caution when stepping over the squeaking floorboards so as not to wake up her son, who was sleeping after his night shift. A few minutes later, her prickly, hoarse smoker's voice rolled through the yard, undoing all her efforts and waking him up long before the arrival of Muradants Andro's truck.

"May your eyes go blind and never see the light of day again!" Manush shouted with abandon. "May your hair fall out in clumps! May your horns grow so long that you get trapped in a bush and never get out! May your tongue grow thorns and your udder a poisonous fungus! May . . ."

"*Ay mer!*"[1] Tsolak yelled over her, throwing open a *shushaband* window.

"*Ha jan!*" Manush reacted, immediately replacing her angry tone with a gentle one.

Tsolak stuck his head out of the window and inhaled the taut morning air still tinged with nighttime frost. A large, round-headed sparrow rose from the branch of an apple tree, shaking off its last ginger-colored leaves. Having made a full circle over the orchard, the sparrow returned, perched on the same branch, and fixed its eyes, full of reproach, on the sleepy Tsolak.

"Look at you!" said Tsolak, suppressing a yawn. "So, my mother's voice didn't scare you, but mine did?"

The sparrow emitted one last baffled chirp, hopped from branch to branch, and disappeared. Tsolak felt around the windowsill for his matches. Without looking, he pulled a cigarette out of the box, rolled it around between his fingers, then collected all the tobacco crumbs that fell into his palm and tossed them over the ledge. He lit up and erupted into a dry cough with his very first puff.

---

1 *Mer* is the simplified version of the Armenian word *mair*, mother.

"You shouldn't smoke on an empty stomach," his mother's squeaky voice reached him from down below.

Tsolak leaned over the windowsill and looked down. Manush stood, a jug of milk pressed to her chest, looking up at her son with adulation.

"What was all that commotion?" he asked.

"The goat made me mad. It's not enough that she barely gives two drops of milk; she also tries to goad me or kick the pail over."

"I'd probably do the same if someone kept cursing me to high heaven."

His mom giggled, covering her mouth with her tanned hand. Tsolak's heart ached with tenderness: he had known and loved this bashful gesture of hers since childhood. She never laughed openly, considering it bad manners, although such scruples never got in the way of being loud and quarrelsome. She was always liable to erupt into endless strings of deafening curses aimed at the good-for-nothing goat that didn't produce enough milk; at the cat that shamelessly stole the dog's food—while the pooch lay around daydreaming, the cat would sneak meat out of its feeding bowl and stash it somewhere, but not before making sure it was properly covered in dirt; at the chickens that, to spite their owner, laid their eggs not in the henhouse but in random places around the garden—and you try and find these silly hens' hiding spots! She rarely stood on ceremony with animals and never thought twice before shouting at them or even kicking them, not hard but definitely mean-spiritedly. Tsolak rarely called her on it, mindful of her peasant temperament. These people have their peculiar ideas about fairness and morality; where the townsfolk will make sure to lay down a mat for safety and cross themselves three times over before proceeding, her kind

124

will plow straight on without sparing themselves, and they will crawl out of their skin to help a stranger in need. But with their uncomplicated and level-headed psyches, they feel no pity or compassion for animals. That's why Manush never really stood on ceremony with them, believing them to be creatures belonging to a lower order and therefore not entitled to any rights. Sometimes Tsolak gently chided her, asking her to show more compassion, but she always cut him off indignantly: "How can you feel sorry for a ewe? You raise it only so that you can eventually eat it! All this talk of being compassionate with animals is the devil's handiwork."

"If Dad could only hear you!"

Mother always shrugged, "And where is your dad? Where exactly is he?"

She'd start crying quietly, furtively wiping her tears with the tips of her headscarf. Tsolak would hug her, show contrition—*ay mer*, come, don't get mad. She didn't.

The only creature with whom his mother had formed a relationship of mutual respect was an owl who, with admirable constancy, sought shelter from bad weather in their attic. Once, having materialized out of thin air, the owl flew in through the narrow attic window and banged its shoulder on the window frame. It tumbled in the air but somehow managed to stay adrift and didn't fall. Having made it to the ceiling beam, it collapsed onto it and hooted dolefully, as if complaining of pain. Manush, setting aside the vinegar-soaked rag with which she was cleaning the attic to keep mildew away, darted to the kitchen, rummaged through the old, long-expired medication left after her husband's death, found some antibacterial tablets and diluted one in some water in case she had to clean the owl's wounds. After brief consideration, she added a second pill—it was expired, but at least two might have some effect. She took a strip of raw meat, went back upstairs, set the meat down on the other side of the ceiling beam and hid behind the trunk. When the owl, with a clumsy side-shuffle, made its way to the meat, Manush got out of her hiding spot as quietly as she could, threw a shawl over the bird, and hugged it tightly in her arms. Quickly feeling its body and ensuring that no bones were broken, she released the bird but not until she had once again hidden behind the trunk—it was important that the owl not see who had grabbed it.

The owl perched on the beam, turning its head this way and that in outrage, looking for the offender, but failing to spot anyone, it calmed down. It waited out the storm and flew off without touching the meat. Since then, it had returned frequently to hide out from bad weather. Whenever Manush saw the skirt of the sky grow dark, she rushed upstairs to the attic, opened both windowpanes, and left a treat—some chicken guts or a handful of chopped beef—in a visible spot. The owl always flew off the moment the weather got better and rarely accepted these offerings, which most likely was what endeared it to Manush. She prized dignity above all other human—and animal—qualities. Judging by how unceremoniously she treated all other animals, the owl must have been the only creature in whom Manush had ever observed this particular trait.

Tsolak knew and loved his mother in all her moods: garrulous, quiet, quarrelsome, tearful, giggly, petty, generous. As she got older, her negative qualities gradually overpowered the positive ones. Her soul grew hardened, and she became indifferent to everything—the world, people, and life in general. Only with her children and grandchildren was she still loving, full of boundless dedication and tenderness, and they reciprocated in full.

Shivering, Tsolak poured some ice-cold water over himself and dried himself with a towel, reveling in the sensation of warmth spreading through his body. He pulled on a fresh shirt and took out his prized leather boots, which he wore sparingly, only for very special occasions. He told his mother he'd be leaving shortly. She was about to ask him where he was going but quickly recalled the occasion and started bustling in the kitchen to get breakfast ready. It was the death anniversary of the old refugee, the great-grandfather of Aleksan's adoptive daughter. When the old man had passed away, Tsolak insisted on paying for the funeral, but Aleksan refused. They paid for it together, meticulously splitting the expenses between the two of them. They went to visit the grave together as well, every year, on the anniversary of his death. They never rehashed their scuffle from years ago. What was there to talk about anyway? Whatever was done was done.

Tsolak frequently remembered his father's words: "Life's too short to remember past insults. Cut off what you don't need and live without looking back." Tsolak always tried to follow this advice.

His father was an amazing person—kind, gentle, and responsive. Animals sensed this and never minded being treated by him. People used to joke that Musheghants Aramais used magic spells to cure animals; there was simply no other way to explain why they took forever to get better when treated by other veterinarians but recovered overnight in Aramais's care despite being treated with the very same medication.

"You need to use your heart for healing. What good are your hands if your heart's not in it?" his father said over and over again.

While Tsolak ate his breakfast, sopping up the last of the sunny-side-up eggs with a piece of bread, his mother sat across from him, smoking and knocking the ash into a cracked saucer.

"You shouldn't smoke on an empty stomach," Tsolak reproached her, using her own words from earlier in the morning.

She flashed him a distracted smile and waved her hand dismissively: "I'll eat later."

After seeing him off, she climbed up to the attic to watch as he walked off with a limp, lifting his shoulder and involuntarily sticking out his elbow every time he stepped on his mangled leg. The old woolen coat, threadbare around the sleeves and the collar, dangled around him pitifully, creasing around the shoulders, and the coat flaps tangled around his knees and impeded his steps. Manush sighed with bitterness; there used to be a time when the same coat barely closed around his midriff.

From the attic window, she could see Berd as if on the palm of her hand. Aleksan's yard is three houses over, and Tsolak will soon be at his gate, calling him; Aleksan will come out at once, and they'll proceed side by side, Aleksan saying something, gesticulating with his healthy right hand, the weak left one pressed to his side, as is his habit, while Tsolak nods in agreement, limping and lifting his shoulder with every step. They will pass by the house of Azinants Tigran, whose eldest daughter, Agapi, is already sitting under the leafless mulberry tree waiting for the evening so that she can go on her invariable stroll; Aleksan and Tsolak will stop to say hello to her through the fence; she won't respond but will flash them her bright smile, and they will continue on their way, comforted by the thought that this world is not completely lost as long as it is warmed by the smile of Azinants Tigran's eldest daughter.

At the fork in the road, they will linger for a few minutes, staring into the blue peaks of the distant mountain pass before turning right and heading up toward the cemetery. While waiting for them to return, Manush will replay in her head how the emaciated herd was heading up the same road on a dank February morning. During the siege, when the cattle had absolutely nothing left to eat, the despairing owners brought the animals to her late husband: "We can't just butcher them, Aramais-jan. If anyone can help them, it's you. Maybe you could give them some medication to help them last till the spring."

"What medication can I give them?" asked her husband helplessly. Manush had wept and begged him not to take the herd to the Molokans who lived on the other side and might have been able to feed the herd until spring, because the road he had to take was constantly shelled. But her husband did not heed her pleas. "I'm going, and that's that. They won't harm me; they'll see that I'm unarmed and just driving some cattle."

Over his father's objections and protestations, Tsolak went with him; after all, they couldn't let him go alone. That day, Manush had stood, clutching the attic window with her frozen fingers, and watched, unblinking, as the herd, accompanied by two shepherd dogs, made its way to the mountain pass. She saw how, out of nowhere, the shooting began; how her son fell first, mowed down by a bullet, and then her husband followed; how the animals, instead of scattering, crowded around the men's bodies, meekly waiting to be slaughtered, and slaughtered they were, down to the very last mournfully mooing cow and pitifully bleating sheep. Manush stood motionlessly by the window, her tear-ravaged eyes staring into the icy night until dawn, when, through the dissipating darkness, she saw that the bodies of her husband and her son had disappeared and finally breathed a sigh of relief. That meant they were still alive and had managed to crawl to safety, she hoped. But there was no getting to them—an animal killed by a bullet can still be used for food, so the area around the massacred herd was under constant fire. The next morning, the unseasonably warm sun melted the snow and unfurled a damp, humid veil over the mountain pass. It wasn't until the evening of the day after that the frost returned, condensing the moisture into an impenetrable fog completely obstructing the view and finally putting an end to the shelling. The fog gave Aleksan and a few others an opening to get up there. When Tsolak was taken to the hospital, his hands were blackened by soil, his nails broken and bleeding, his shattered and swollen leg barely attached by a few strings of tendon and muscle. In his delirium, he talked incessantly about dragging his father's body into a gully and waiting for help that he knew would never arrive, about trying to dig a grave for him in the frozen, unyielding soil and only just managing to cover his face and chest but leaving the legs unburied. What if jackals got to the body and gnawed them off, he raved and kept trying to get up, to go back and finish burying his father.

Much later, after the delirious fever had passed, he fell silent; he said nothing and suffered from insomnia. It was as if he had unlearned how to sleep. He never touched meat again—he couldn't forget the stench emanating from the dead herd rotting in the rays of the inexplicably warm winter sun.

When she spots Aleksan and Tsolak back at the fork in the road, Manush rushes downstairs, grunting from the pain in her aching joints, and resumes her housework. Tsolak never admitted to his friend that he hadn't been the one to set the trap in his yard, and he forbade his mother to say anything about it—I am the man of the house, I will bear the responsibility for it. Manush cried at first but ended up acquiescing without much of a fight; if her son wished to answer for her in this world, so be it—she'd be on her own in the next one.

"Life's too short to hold on to quarrels," her late husband liked to say. "Cut off what you don't need and live without looking back over your shoulder." That's exactly what Tsolak did, but she, for her part, failed to do the same. She chose not to. She let her soul harden and her heart grow cold. She never forgave her husband for disobeying her wishes and willingly walking to his own death. "Was your silly lack of judgment worth my loneliness and tears?" she kept asking, going over in her mind the unbearable years of having to raise the little ones all by herself, with no help from Tsolak, whose recovery was long and difficult. "Do you really think it was worth our son's well-being?" She kept tormenting herself with this question, the answer to which she was destined never to find.

Stroll

Azinants Agapi always went on her strolls toward
evening. She walked down the sloping street paved
with small pebbles until it ended, and then she
turned right, toward the spring. She did not stop there—she
would drink her fill on the way back.

She passed by the small shops and workshops, pausing by
each one. The greengrocer was awkwardly sorting through
the highly perishable cilantro and watercress; the grocer was
pouring raisins and nuts into paper bags. The tailor's sewing
machine was chattering, and the smell of a hot iron wafted
through the air. In the shoe repair shop, an old woman in a
dark headdress sat, bashfully hiding her foot clad in a plain
stocking while the cobbler repaired her boots.

Nobody remained indifferent to Agapi's visit.

"Hello, Agapi-jan," the greengrocer greeted her.

"May Jesus Christ be your protector, Agapi-jan," said
the grocer.

"How are you feeling, Agapi-jan?" inquired the tailor.

"All will be well, Agapi-jan," chimed in the cobbler.

The old lady shook her head and sighed. Agapi smiled and
continued her journey. Past the stone houses, past the uneven
fences, past the yapping yard dogs, past the empty autumnal

orchards: once the quinces and frost-kissed persimmons were gathered, the trees would slumber till spring.

Her journey ended at the stone bridge. She leaned against the old railing, listening to the voice of the river. These days it is hoarse and faint, its words incomprehensible. On the left there is an old cemetery, on the right, a narrow path leading up to the bald summit of Khali-Kar. When she was a little girl, she used to climb up there every day. "Agaaapi," her mother would call, "be careful, don't go near the cliff."

"I won't," Agapi would promise, and then she would stand right at the edge, taking in the voice of the river. It was strong and clear back then, its every word like an entire song.

"It doesn't behoove a girl to run away from home," her mother would scold her.

Agapi would promise that she would never again run away, but run away she did. She had the face of an angel: big translucent eyes, fluffy eyelashes, thick wavy hair.

"She will grow up to be a beauty," said the neighbors.

"What matters most is that she grows up happy," her mother would counter.

Agapi knew everything a seven-year-old girl should know about happiness: loving parents, delicious food, a warm bed. A younger brother and sister, a dog named Vilka. The only thing she didn't know was why unripe apples tasted so much better than ripe ones. And why the adults forbade her to eat the apples while they were still sour, forcing her to wait until they ripened to boring sweetness. She did not like to wait, which is why she would pick the apples off the trees and climb all the way to the summit of Khali-Kar, to listen to the river.

Her family was one of those circumvented by the war: no home destroyed, no men killed in action, no women kidnapped or vanished. They held on to each other, helped their neighbors, visited the chapel: her mother would light candles and thank God. "Astvats-jan, don't consider it too much that we're luckier than many others." While she prayed, Agapi and her younger sister, standing on their tiptoes, studied the icon of the Holy Mother.

"Why is she so sad?" her sister would whisper.

"Maybe someone's upset her," Agapi would respond.

Their mother would shush them and continue with her thanksgiving, "Astvats-jan, Astvats-jan."

Agapi would raise her eyes to the chapel's window, from which a narrow beam of light fell on the uneven floor. On sunny days weightless dust particles swarmed in it; on rainy days doleful shadows floated.

The war started when she was eight and abated when she was thirteen. The relatives were cautiously happy: it has spared us, it has spared us. Within a year, both of her aunts died from a serious blood disorder. Her mother followed, for the same reason. And one day Agapi crossed over the threshold of reality to the other side, never to return. Her younger brother and sister remained, and the decrepit dog Vilka, and her father turned grey and old overnight. Nobody talked about the war in Agapi's family, perhaps because they knew everything about it. That it has a tendency to start but never ends. That it destroys houses and takes away the men, and then, when it calms down, it inflicts incurable diseases upon the women. After having its way with the adults, it takes the young people who can't handle their fears and pushes them over the edge of sanity. The war marks everybody with unique stamps; it doesn't let anyone slip by.

Azinants Agapi returns from her stroll late in the evening. Passing from one streetlamp to the next, she freezes for a

second in the circle of light. On moonlit nights weightless dust
particles swarm there, on foggy nights doleful shadows float.

She remembers nothing and recognizes nobody. The whole
meaning of her existence boils down to these everyday strolls:
down the sloping street, past the shops and workshops, toward
the old bridge. Standing, as she leans against the railings, and
listening to the river. Drinking from the spring on the way
back. And waiting for the spring, when sour unripe apples
will appear once again. Agapi has finally learned why they
are more delicious than the ripe ones, but she has no way to
explain it to others.

Boots

"**D**oes it pinch a lot?" Makarants Kolik craned his neck to get a better look at Nunufar's foot. Then he immediately checked himself and turned away, scolding himself for lack of tact. Nunufar folded her leg under her and frowned, feeling her stocking snagged by a splinter of the crudely made bench. She swiped her finger over the nick: it didn't seem torn. If it were a nylon stocking, it would have run right away, but a cotton one shouldn't. And even if it did, she would simply mend it in such a way that the stocking would be as good as new.

"Let me show you," she took the boot from the cobbler and pointed to the base of the zipper. "Here is where it presses and hurts. As you know yourself, with diabetes any little injury causes pain."

Kolik, nodding, went to work right away. While he was extracting the zipper, bending low over the boot and constantly clearing his throat, Nunufar sat with her hands folded in her lap and looked around at the drab interior of the shop: dusty shelves piled high with shoes, repaired or waiting for their turn; brushes sticky with glue; little jars full of God-knows-what; threads; various awls and knives; desiccated and cracked polish in antediluvian tin boxes.

There was a poster of yet another insipid presidential candidate staring at her from the wall—she had seen so many that she had lost count, and they all seemed to be competing to outdo each other in shamelessness and dishonesty. Nunufar read the clumsy name of the candidate's party ("More Prosperous Republic"), then took a minute to study his heavy square jaw and tiny sly eyes. "You, shameless mug!" she thought and turned to Kolik with indignation, "Why did you hang this bonehead on your wall?"

He followed her glance and scoffed, "He covers the crack. He's good for something, at least."

"I have some plaster at home. I will bring it over and repair the crack, but take him down. He doesn't deserve the honor."

Kolik obligingly tore the poster off the wall, crumpled it, and threw it under the woodstove to use with kindling later. Nunufar looked on with unconcealed satisfaction. When the lump of crumpled paper bounced off a log, she didn't spare the effort it required to stand up and, carefully stepping on her unshod heel, pick it up and tossed it back under the stove.

Kolik missed all this because he had stepped outside to have a smoke.

"You are coughing, but you still smoke," Nunufar managed to comment wryly, loudly sniffing the air with her nostrils and distorting her face as if the cigarette smoke was already inside her lungs.

"I can smoke if I want! I am not a child—I'm fifty years old!" the cobbler made a feeble attempt to justify himself.

"And I care because . . .?"

Kolik shuffled his feet tentatively, not daring to contradict Nunufar (respect for elders trumped everything else), and in the end held his tongue. The tailor poked his head out of the neighboring shop and pulled a cigarette out of Kolik's pack. Kolik lit a match for him.

"Eh, I wish you at least showed some conscience, Arto!" exclaimed Nunufar.

The tailor, plump and broad-shouldered, coughed and threw up his hands with an unexpectedly childish and seemingly helpless expression in his bright blue eyes, "Where would I get a conscience, Nunufar-moqir?"[1]

"So, when God was distributing conscience, he deliberately skipped you?"

"You are right, he deliberately skipped me. But then he felt guilty about it, so he bestowed beauty upon me twice over," countered the unflappable Arto, who was infamous in Berd for his indisputable, and one might say crushing, lack of good looks.

"You are quite attractive—perhaps a bit deformed and pock-marked, but who isn't?" Nunufar generously assured him. Then, deeming her comeback insufficient, added, "At least you're safe from being jinxed—the evil eye cannot touch ugliness."

"*Vah*,[2] mama-jan," snickered Kolik.

Attracted by his laughter, the young tailor's apprentice poked his head out of the shop, but then got bashful and disappeared.

"Nunufar-moqir, you really ought to be the minister of foreign affairs," Arto joked.

"With you, our otherwise patchy foreign diplomacy would be elevated to an unprecedented level!" added Kolik.

Nunufar sized them up with judging eyes. "They are mocking me, two boneheads."

---

1 *Moqir*, an abbreviated form of the Armenian word *moraquir*, literally "mother's sister" (maternal aunt). It is used to address not only one's aunts but also older women with whom one is on familiar terms.

2 Equivalent to "oh my goodness," a generic expression encompassing a broad range of meanings from amazement to exasperation.

However, she couldn't help it—she also broke into a smile.

Having finished his smoke, Kolik went back to work. He wielded his needle, shook his head, and chuckled kindheartedly. Nunufar sat with her hands folded in her lap and her lips pressed into a thin line. In response to the cobbler's every giggle her face would light up with a momentary smile and then go dark again. Her profile resembled a big crow: dark-skinned, hawk-nosed, with inquisitive, lively, coal-black eyes. Under her tightly tied kerchief there was an outline of a heavy knot of hair: Vayinants Nunufar hasn't cut her hair in forty years. One day she just covered her head with a kerchief, and nobody has seen her head uncovered since. Rumor has it that she has never once washed her hair in all those years, but that is unlikely: the odor of hair unwashed for almost half a century would be different from how Nunufar smells. She smells of simple soap, dried fruit, and leavened dough—that is, of everything that ordinary Berd grandmothers smell of.

Forty years ago, having saved enough money, Nunufar sent her oldest son to the big city to become a dental technician. That was how she kept the promise she had given to her dying husband, who held firmly to his belief in the power and importance of receiving a city education. Her younger ones, the six-year-old twins, remained in her care. She received the bad news while at work. She was preparing to go home when the phone rang and the telegraph operator, in a voice faint with horror, read her a telegram reporting that there had been a terrible tragedy the day before: a trolleybus had fallen into a lake in the city, killing many people. Her Vachagan was among them.[3]

---

3 On September 16, 1976, in Yerevan, the capital of Armenia, a trolleybus fell into a lake. Forty-six of the ninety-two passengers were rescued; the other forty-six drowned.

Nunufar could not quite picture what a trolleybus was. When she reached the city, the first thing she did was ask to be shown one. She could not quite grasp how such a big and sturdy vehicle managed to fall into a lake. "Wouldn't those things that tie it to the wires keep it in place?" she asked a young doctor who, without lifting his eyes for fear of meeting hers, was writing out Vachagan's death certificate. The doctor did not argue with her, he just tentatively shrugged his shoulders: things happen. After writing out the certificate, he measured her blood pressure, packed two pills for her to take with her, and made sure that she took another two right there. Nunufar touched his hand when saying goodbye: thank you, sonny. A week later, she received Vachagan's body in a sealed coffin with a small glass window over where his face was supposed to be. She tried to see her son through the cloudy window but didn't succeed. She didn't cry during the funeral: she could not convince herself that it was her Vachagan inside the coffin.

On the fortieth day after the funeral a strange woman knocked at her door. Refusing Nunufar's offer to come inside, at least as far as the hallway, and instead standing at the threshold and shifting from one foot to the other, she told Nunufar that the night before she had dreamed of two men, one very young, almost a child, no more than seventeen, and the other one older, with grey temples and rays of wrinkles around his eyes, and that in her dream they had asked her to go to faraway Berd and let Vayinants Nunufar know that she need not worry about them, that they were living in a spacious and brightly lit house with views of the sunset, just like she had always wanted, and so in the mornings it was not too hot to enjoy breakfast, and they could have supper while admiring the flickering hem of the sky haphazardly tossed over the blue mountains; the young one used those exact unusual words, the

woman said, shaking her head perplexedly, and then added that
he also wanted her to convey that Nunufar should not be upset
with him for dying too early and that she should take good
care of the younger sons because he was uneasy about them.
After narrating her dream, the woman said goodbye and left
at once, refusing even a cup of coffee because she was afraid to
miss the intercity bus. Nunufar put together a package of food,
ran panting to the station, and managed to hand it through the
bus window to the stranger at the last second. It wasn't until
the bus disappeared from sight that she realized she hadn't
asked the woman her name or address. After she came home,
she cried for several days, and finally believing that her son was
dead and reconciling herself to the thought, she tied a black
kerchief around her head.

She spent her entire life fretting over her twin sons, mindful
of her dead husband's warning, and didn't let them go to the
city, instead making them apprentice locally to become electri-
cians; she preferred that they repair wires rather than live away
from her. The war started when her sons turned twenty, and
while both had already completed their military service, they
volunteered to fight on the front. Nunufar cried her eyes out
imploring them not to do it: "There are other people who can
fight, why you?"

But her sons held steadfast: "If not us, then who?"

Then, urged by unbearable despair and pain, she implored
them, "You can't both leave me: one of you should stay with me!"

One of the twins—later she had trouble recalling which
one—responded to her with the cold rage of a young reckless
heart, "Then you pick which one of us stays!"

That is how Nunufar failed to protect her sons.

"Nunufar-moqir, try it again, it shouldn't bother you now."
Kolik handed her the boot.

Lost in her memories, she had a hard time recovering from the stream of her thoughts and stared at the boot uncomprehendingly for a few seconds, but then she caught herself and accepted it, turning it in her hands and peering into the invisible stitch. She stood up, walked around the workshop, stepping on her bare foot, and stood for a while over the woodfire stove. She suddenly bent over, opened the furnace's flap, and threw the crumpled poster into the fire, remembering to comment acidly: "They all have the same shameless face!" She watched the poster smolder, engulfed in the messy, bitter smoke.

"They won't even burn properly!" she scoffed.

Kolik scratched the back of his head: "You really don't like them, do you?"

"Why would I? Would we be mourning our children if this wretched country were ruled by decent people?"

Kolik timidly nodded in agreement. He indignantly turned down her attempt to pay him. Nunufar promised to bake him *gata* to show her gratitude. She put her shoes on, bashfully turning her back to him. She touched his hand before saying goodbye: thank you, sonny.

"Does it still hurt?" Kolik shouted after her, poking his head out of the workshop.

She turned and waved her hand: "Don't worry, *tsavd tanem*.[4] Not anymore."

---

4 See footnote on page 45.

Choice

———

"When God deprives a man of one quality, he overcompensates with another. That is what he did for our Arto: he did not grant him beauty but instead rewarded him with the bottomless gift of gab that makes you want to plug your ears!" Avakants Mishik, catching the eye of the tailor's apprentice, winked and turned back to the stove, making sure that the simmering coffee did not boil over from the *jezve*. The apprentice, a gawky young man with convincing-looking fuzz over his upper lip, smiled with embarrassment and, in an attempt to conceal his timidity, redoubled the zeal with which he served the plates with the crumbly *gata* that Vayinants Nunufar had sent along earlier that morning. The tailor, the subject of the conversation, folded his huge shapeless hands over his chest and leaned against the back of his chair; it creaked pitifully and shook under his weight.

"Don't mistake lightning for a lightning bug, Mishik! I'm not chatty, I'm eloquent! And let's not point fingers at those who indeed talk too much, right, Masis-jan!" Arto turned to his apprentice. Masis, completely mortified, froze over the plate.

"Now why would you put the kid on the spot like that?" Kolik rushed to his defense.

"Well, I think I haven't been a child for some time now!" exclaimed Masis, his voice treacherously breaking with anxiety. His last words were drowned out by approving laughter.

"He got us, oh, he got us good!" Arto slapped his sides, his big, round belly shaking. The chair on which he sat shook, threatening to fall apart. The cobbler laughed, half squatting and screeching. Only the grocer retained his feigned composure, although it was clear from the trembling corners of his lips that he would not last long.

"Are you making fun of the kid again?" the greengrocer poked in his head, provoking another outburst of mirth with his question.

"Suro, he hasn't been a kid for a while now, for at least five minutes!" choked out Kolik.

"Does he have a certificate to prove it?"

"Of course he has! Stamped, notarized, and everything!"

"To hell with you all!" Masis, demonstrating with his whole demeanor that he was not much bothered by the conversation, took the last piece of *gata* from the box, bit it in half, and started chewing. When someone offered him a cup of coffee, he accepted it reluctantly, as if doing everyone a favor. His facial expression remained impassive as he took a sip of the hot beverage, and then he suddenly started coughing. He bent over and pushed his palms into his knees. Unable to overcome the choking fit, he straightened up sharply and headed toward the exit: there, in cold November air, he would be able to catch his breath. Arto, with an agility surprising in such an ample body, jumped up and ran after him. His shoulder caught the door frame and he nearly fell over the threshold. He firmly hugged Masis, grabbed him by his jaw, and tilted his head backward to allow air into his lungs.

"Breathe, sonny. Don't panic. Breathe."

Masis opened his mouth wide, gulping air, and his entire body felt the iron grip on his chest loosen. He breathed tensely, greedily inhaling the prickly, frosty air. A flock of doves, turbulently chirping, circled over his head. Berd's sky stood coarse, cracked, depressingly indifferent as it always did in the fall.

"That's because winter is coming," Masis thought, wiping away the welling tears.

Mishik brought him some water. "Drink!"

"I'm fine."

"Drink, I said!"

He took a couple sips, returned the glass. He turned his eyes from worried Mishik to Arto. The distressed greengrocer hovered in the doorway of the shop.

"The coffee's probably gone cold," Masis ventured guiltily.

"To hell with coffee, what matters most is *jansakhutyun*.[1] Is your cough getting better?"

"It is."

"A change of climate might do you good," the greengrocer chimed in.

Masis did not argue. He stepped aside, letting the older men go in first. He took a paper napkin from his pocket, coughed, and wiped his lips. A droplet of blood appeared on the white surface. He hastily crumpled the napkin and hid it in his pocket. God forbid they notice, they will drag him to the doctor. Last time Arto turned the entire hospital upside down, waving the x-ray image around like a weapon. And what can the doctors do? They can't restore burned lungs to full capacity! There is nothing to be done about them anymore, and Arto of

---

1 "Health" in local Armenian dialect.

course understands it better than anybody. That was why he threatened the doctors with the x-ray images—driven by his humiliating powerlessness to change the unchangeable.

MASIS HAD LONG FORGOTTEN the joy of breathing in a full chest of air without worrying about choking fits. He started having them during the war, which he barely remembered: he was too little when it arrived in his native village of Karin-Tak. The village was besieged, weapons were blasting, fires were set, and there was incessant bombing. The blockade starved the villagers, the drinking wells were poisoned. But the village would not surrender. After countless failed attacks, the enemy settled on deception: they announced a two-day truce so the people could bury their dead. At dawn the enemy advanced to storm the village. Since Masis's house was located on the very outskirts, it was first in line to be taken. His father had an old rifle and about twenty bullets. Putting aside three bullets—for himself, his wife, and his little son—he rushed from window to window, returning fire in such a way as to give the enemy the impression that there were several people putting up the resistance. Convinced, they resorted to using hand grenade launchers. By the time help arrived, the house was on fire, and his mother and father, who had locked themselves in the cellar, tried to beat back the unbearable heat by pouring sauerkraut brine over themselves and their son. His father had no bullets left except the three he had set aside. He was loading them into the gun when rescuers arrived.

All that Masis remembered from the massive war was the acrid smoke eating out his eyes and his lungs. He also remembered a huge man, who broke down the heavy door with his shoulder, gathered Masis into his arms, and carried him out of the blazing cellar. The air outside was so tight and unwieldy that it scratched the roof of his mouth and stuck in his throat. The man pressed Masis's back tightly against his body, grabbed his chin, tilting back his head to make breathing easier. From the altitude of the man's height Masis saw their yard, piled with shapeless bales, and a burning orchard. Behind the sharp-edged trunk of the mulberry tree, a bearded man was crouching and staring at him, his head twisted at an odd angle. Masis's savior pushed the man to the ground with his shoulder and, after the man fell onto his side, grabbed him by the collar and dragged him toward the bales. Then it became clear that those were not bales but corpses strewn around the yard. "If it weren't for you, we would have had many losses," Arto would sometimes say to Masis's father.

His father always shrugged his shoulders in response.

"And if it weren't for you, they would have killed so many of us!"

When Masis turned eight, Arto brought him to live at his house: the doctors insisted that Berd's mild climate would do him good and reduce the boy's choking fits, which got progressively worse with every passing year. Masis was reluctant to go, but his father convinced him.

"Arto will take you on as an apprentice: you'll learn a trade when school is out. Having extra skills never hurt anyone."

"I can learn to be a tailor here!"

"What matters most is not the trade but your health. And think about Arto, son. You have your mother and me and your younger brothers. How do you think Arto feels? With you, he won't be as lonely."

IT'S BEEN FIVE YEARS now since Masis moved to Berd. During the holidays he visits his family in Karin-Tak, and the rest of the time he lives with Arto. On Tuesdays, when

Avakants Mishik visits the old *khachkar*, he fills in for him
in his grocery store. On Fridays and Sundays, he tutors the
cobbler's daughter in math. He adamantly refuses to accept
money. The men love him to pieces and have taken to calling
him "the son of the battalion." They parent him awkwardly
and inexpertly. Masis treats their pedagogical endeavors with
understanding but has now developed the habit of snapping
back. Thirteen is a serious age, they must understand that.

Sometimes his longing for his family becomes so unbearable
that Masis wants to hitchhike home right away. But he never
does that because he doesn't want to upset Arto and his own
parents, for whom his health is the most important thing.
"I would agree not to see you for years if it meant that your
burned lungs would recover," his mother once said as she was
seeing him off to Berd yet again. After saying that she burst
into tears and hugged him so tightly that his father had to
unclench her fingers and help his son break free. Masis sometimes imagines that they are still there, in that burning house,
and his mother, coughing and choking from the acrid smoke, is
still rushing back and forth between the pickling jars, soaking
the three of them with the brine, which dries immediately,
leaving a scratchy crust on their bodies. He imagines that his
father, having used all the other bullets, rolls the last three
around in his palm for a long, unbearable eternity, and then
with a restrained and decisive move pulls the bolt of his rifle
and loads it.

Once he confessed to Masis that the most painful thing he
ever faced was that choice. "I never would have surrendered
alive. And I could not leave you behind for them to torture. I
had no fear of death, no despair, no doubt. The only thing that
tortured me was that choice. The whole time I was fighting

back from inside the house, I kept thinking only about one thing: which one of you I would need to shoot first: you or your mother."

Masis knows about the war exactly what any dweller of borderlands does: once it starts, it tends to never end. The war will spread slowly, poisoning with its foul breath everything in its way. One morning it will unfailingly appear on the threshold of your house and present you with the only possible choice: to leave, taking with you everybody you love.

The Heart

Zabel used to say, "Don't lie on your left side, it is bad for the heart—both yours and mine, because I also lie on my left side when you do."

"You work in a hospital and still believe in this nonsense!" Arto used to gripe, turning onto his right side.

"I don't believe it, but my great-grandmother taught us when we were kids not to lie on the heart side," Zabel tried to justify herself.

She liked to sleep "shell-style," as she referred to it: if he turned on his side, so did she, hugging him from behind, clinging to him vulnerably and breathing into his back.

"You've really grown yourself some belly," Zabel used to say. "If I were an ant, my whole life would not be enough to crawl from one side of it to the other; I would age and die by the time I got to this spot," and she would poke him in his belly button.

He would squirm—he was ticklish—and she would laugh uproariously and loudly.

"I would crawl right in here and surrender my soul to God, my duty fulfilled."

"Don't say that!" Arto would grow somber.

"That you're fat?"

"No, that you'll surrender your soul to God!"

"Oh sweetie! My sweet darling!"

"What?"

"I love you, that's what."

ZABEL USED TO SAY, "Can you imagine, if on that day you had stopped not at my office but at Tsivinants Ninik's? She's also a great nurse, with a light touch—you can't even feel it when she gives you a shot—and she is so much prettier than me. Right, much prettier?" she would say, feeling resentful and getting angry.

Arto tried to keep a straight face to mask his amused delight.

"Yes, I got unlucky."

"Dumbo!" she would flare up.

"I don't know anyone more beautiful than you!" he would rush to correct himself.

"Really?"

"Really."

"Fine," Zabel would sigh, like a child who is all cried out, "but imagine if you hadn't stopped by. We would've never met and fallen in love. We would've never gotten married. We would've never lived in this brick house. I would've never fed you this dinner—it's delicious, isn't it?"

"Well, how should I put it? It's OK . . ." Arto would start again.

"Just OK? Is that why you are having a second helping? Put it back, you ingrate!"

He would gather her into his arms and kiss the honeyed groove behind her collarbone.

"It's delicious, you silly goose, delicious!"

"That's more like it!"

ZABEL USED TO SAY, "How can one particular, fairly compact, and, relative to the universe, tiny person occupy the whole space of my life? How, and more importantly, why? Perhaps out of stubbornness. From the sheer desire to be difficult or, worse yet, to do damage!" and she'd give him a look that made Arto's heart ache with tenderness and love.

"Whereas I listen to you and understand what happiness is when and if it finds you. I adore you, my one particular, fairly compact, and, relative to the universe, tiny reason for happiness," he would whisper.

THEY MET DURING a frigid January. Arto, who had caught a very nasty cold and developed a backache, went to see a doctor, where he was directed to the procedure rooms for the prescribed injections, and there she was—tenderly rosy-cheeked, with shiny chestnut-colored eyes and such a thick mop of red hair that it was a wonder she managed to shove all of it under her nurse's cap. Overcome by embarrassment, he offered an excuse and tried to make a quick exit, but she, sensing the true cause of his sudden shyness, informed him that the other nurse was also young, and that he had nowhere to go. She warned him honestly that the injection would hurt because, on top of medication, he was prescribed vitamins, and those were always painful.

"Will you manage?" she asked.

"I've handled worse."

He lay down, barely lowering his pants. She tried to lower them farther, but he did not let her—stick it here or not at all. After the injections, which indeed turned out to be painful, she did not let him stand up.

"Please remain lying down for at least ten minutes, that's what you're supposed to do."

He obeyed, but not before pulling up his pants with a groan. She laughed.

"You are so shy."

"Well, I am who I am," he mumbled.

By the end of his treatment, they seemed to know everything about each other. She was from Karabakh, from a village called Karin-Tak, renting a room at Zhemanzhants Katinka's house ("Do you know why they are called Zhemanzhants? Their French grandfather was quite a glutton, and, at any time of the day, whenever he was called upon he would respond, *'Je mange!'* That means 'I am eating!' You people from Berd are so funny!" He would laugh, "Well, what did you think?")

He was taking night classes at the agriculture school but was making some extra cash sewing trousers at the tailor's shop. (He would say, "Don't mind my clumsy hands, I'm really a good tailor." She, "People praise you a lot, I know." He, "Really, a lot?" She, "Yep! Why are you blushing?" He, "Why are you embarrassing me with all this praise?")

He proposed to her in April, and they got married in June, barely getting through May, and they only waited that long out of respect for her great-grandmother, who insisted that nobody should get married in May because nothing good ever comes out of it since it is *"maiis-vaiis,"*[1] after all.

At the end of summer, Zabel went to visit her family, and two weeks later her village was surrounded. Arto enlisted as a volunteer, and the military troops spent weeks trying in vain to get through to her village. Once, after heavy fighting, they managed to break through the enemy siege, to find themselves briefly approaching Karin-Tak before being pushed back. Through his binoculars, Arto could make out the

---

1 *Mais*, May in Armenian. *Vais*, from the Armenian exclamation *vai* which means "alas."

carefully washed laundry—baby onesies, leggings, hats, and diapers—flapping in the wind in the yards of the houses that had survived the bombing. He saw how thin chimney smoke coiled up to the sky as the housewives lit up their stoves to cook dinner before the next round of shooting began. He saw men lowering themselves to the ground to avoid the bullets while scampering from house to house. The dogs were silent, but the birds were chirping, and the roosters kept crowing, their frenzied dissonance bringing chaos to the otherwise tranquil September afternoon.

Fiercely buzzing, the bees swarmed in the air, the strong aroma of the field flowers made him dizzy, and far away the river sang, awakened by the abrupt morning shower. Arto put away his binoculars, feeling a slight sense of irritation: nature's beauty could be so meaningless in time of war!

They finally reached Karin-Tak at the end of the fall. All the surrounding areas were lightly dusted with night snow and engulfed in an impenetrable fog, which provided cover for them to reach their destination, breaking through the enemy blockade without suffering any losses. As they were approaching the village, on the very edge of a small ravine, they stumbled across black, burned, mutilated corpses. There was no time to distinguish friend from foe, so they took everyone. They would bury their own as well as the enemy, since the other side hadn't. Taking their weapons with them, they barely managed to drag the corpses to the edge of town; toward daybreak the fog dissolved into bone-chilling precipitation, turning the ground covered with grainy snow into an impassable mush. Lining up the bodies—the villagers would sort them out later—they prepared to go on when Arto stopped in his tracks. He noticed the familiar red curls on one of the corpses near the edge. He got on his knees, grabbed a palmful of snow, and, fighting a feeling of dread, cleaned the mud-caked hair and the face made unrecognizable by soot. And then he uttered a howl—horrifying and primal—not yet understanding the sorrow that had befallen him, but already suffocating from its unbearable burden. This was his Zabel: with short hair, emaciated—skin and bones, in ill-fitting military boots and an unwieldy man's pea jacket. "My love, ah, my love," he called, barely moving his tongue, feeling how his frosty breath was fettering his lips. For some reason he unbuttoned the collar of her shirt and pressed his forehead to the groove behind her collarbone. He noticed in her frozen fingers a patch of cloth and pulled it out with difficulty, recognizing the scrap of a nurse's bag. He lay down, curled up, in the way she liked to do, and closed his eyes. Zabel's great-grandmother had it all wrong—on the right side the heart ached as much as on the left, if not more.

Silence

The water had to settle first. Painstakingly rinsing out the water carafe, Ninik filled it up to the brim, covered it, and put it in a cool spot to rest. The old silver coin clinked on the bottom, purifying and blessing the water. Heating the butter till it began to gently smoke and setting it to rest until it developed a thin white film on top, Ninik cut the crude country bread into thick slices and measured a cup of *pokhindz*. She waited for the fire to get going in the stove and put on a kettle, which quickly came to a boil, spewing steam through its chipped spout and blowing a hoarse whistle. It didn't require much work: all she had to do was mix the boiling water with tap water, add some salt, pour in the grain carefully to avoid clumping, stir everything with a wooden spatula, put it on the stove, let it sit until it began puffing and then let it cook for another minute or two. Having removed the little pan with *pokhindz* from the heat, Ninik wiped the sizzling hot top of the stove and arranged the bread slices on it. While the bread was toasting, she brewed some thyme infusion and brought soft goat cheese from the cellar. She cut a piece of beeswax honey, trying not to press it too hard with the knife so the honey wouldn't seep out. She covered a large nickel tray with a linen napkin. She stacked the crisped bread in a neat pile and propped it with a cup of tea to prevent it from tumbling over; next to it, she positioned the saucers with cheese and honey. She transferred the *pokhindz* into a bowl, made small furrows on its surface with the edge of the spoon and poured in the cooled melted butter—it melted again and trickled in joyous rivulets all over the porridge. She carried the tray, stepping carefully and constantly watching her feet. She had to push open the kitchen door with her hip. The tea spilled, making two dark stains on the napkin. Ninik scolded herself for the memory lapse: every morning she tells herself to prop the door open and then forgets. The floorboards under her feet emitted a lingering squeak. Picked up by a draft, the old curtain swayed in the windows, letting in the stingy autumn light. The ancient clock—there was no learning its actual age anymore—ticked with strain, measuring out time.

Her mother had told her that the clock was left behind by Zhamants Vaghinak, who had come almost a century ago to ask for the hand of her great-grandmother Anahit. He was eighteen then, she—fifteen; he was a sturdy broad-shouldered fellow, a true *pekhlevan*,[1] she—Berd's greatest beauty. But she turned him down, although she liked him and had promised him the day before, in front of the water spring, that she would marry him and had even given him her photograph. For some reason, she turned him down, and he left insulted, but did not take back the clock because who on earth would take back a gift. He never spoke to her or so much as returned her greeting again, crossing to the other side of the street or turning in the opposite direction when they ran into each other, and later he married Mailants Varinka, had two sons, and was killed during the First World War. In his breast pocket, in addition

---

1 A heroic figure who possesses enormous strength.

to his children's photographs, they discovered Anahit's faded photo that smelled of man sweat and tobacco. Varinka received it along with his death certificate, brought it over to Anahit, and handed it to her across the threshold. She refused to enter the house and only bitterly remarked that even in death he loved Anahit more than his own wife; she had never doubted it because she felt and knew it in her heart. In Ninik's family it was customary to say that the clock was as old as Zhamants Vaghinak's broken heart, and every time Ninik heard its uneven chiming, she couldn't help but think, lo and behold, great-grandma is no longer alive, neither is Vaghinak, yet the witness of their unmaterialized life together is still here, measuring out time, dispassionate and detached, unperturbed by sad events a century ago.

The wind, having run wild all night, was knocking around the wooden shutters and whistling in the chimney, chasing the sweet-smelling smoke of burning wood into the house. Sensing the approach of sleet and rain, the rooster crowed in vexation, and a silent flock of yellow siskins perched on the neighboring fence: when the frost arrived, they always took off from their homesteads and migrated to the river delta, to winter in warmth there. Ninik smiled, noting to herself the gloomy concentration with which the siskins were staring ahead as if seeing something that neither she nor the noisy rooster nor the wind, chilled and smelling of the icy breath of the mountains, was destined to figure out.

Her mother was lying in a remote room, the brightest and warmest in the house, with views of a small cypress grove. As a child, Ninik would often escape to that grove; she would stand beneath the trees, inhaling their spicy pinewood smell, rolling the rough cones in her palms, biting into them and grimacing when she tasted their unbearable bitterness; she would then sniff her fingers for a long time, resurrecting in her memory the moist scent of earth covered with flaky pine needles. When her mother got very sick, Ninik carried her in her arms into that room, crying in terror as she stepped—her mother was so emaciated that Ninik could see her bones. She was practically weightless, her thin and lifeless skin glistened through her thin gray hair, her eyes had lost their sparkle, and her once-beautiful face, completely disfigured by mourning, expressed nothing but bottomless grief. Ninik remembered her completely differently: she was willful and unyielding, never acknowledging anybody else's opinion or her own errors. In Berd, they called her "*tkhamard aghchik*," a man-girl, and it was unclear whether there was more respect or condemnation in that moniker. Every inhabitant of Berd had his own opinion on the subject. Her mother raised her three daughters on her own because once, after an intense argument with her husband, she kicked him out and never let him back in again. Having cut off all communication not only with him but his entire family, she refused all help, turned down any money, and did not pick up the baskets of delectable fruits that they left outside her door: her mother-in-law had a huge orchard, in which she managed to grow things that never grew in that harvest-stingy terrain. Nevertheless, Ninik never forbade her daughters to socialize with their father's relatives and even let them stay over for several days at a time, although she never asked how they had spent their time and cut short all their attempts to tell her. She ruthlessly discarded all the gifts they received from their father's side. Ninik could never forget how her older sister sobbed when her mother forced her to take off the expensive jeans she had received for her fifteenth birthday. "But you'll never be able to buy me these!" she cried, begging her mother not to take them away from her. "Of course I won't—I can't afford these on a teacher's salary," her mother responded with stony calm, and took the jeans to dispose of them in the outhouse. Ninik's older sister came down with a fever, and their mother faithfully nursed her back to health, but only shrugged in response to the other daughters' bitter reproaches that she was the cause of their sister's sickness. "Don't even try, I will always get my way."

They never found out the source of their parents' quarrel; by the time the girls were old enough to want to find out what had transpired, their father was dead, consumed by an incurable illness, and their mother responded to all questions with stony silence.

The two older daughters, unable to deal with her difficult temper, got married straight out of school. Both cut off communication, lived in town, called home rarely and reluctantly, and treated their mother with respect but without affection. When they found out that she was sick, they sent money but never expressed any desire to visit. For her part, Ninik never asked them. She knew her sisters wouldn't come because they both had inherited their mother's unyielding disposition, her inability to compromise, and her cold, destructive anger; that is why they lived nursing and feeding their anger and recognizing nothing beyond it. Only Ninik grew up kind and gentle like her quiet and compliant father; she was always nearby, never contradicted her mother, and did everything to please her. She even looked like her father: tall, dark-haired, and dark-eyed, with adorable dimples on her cheeks. Sometimes her mother held this fact against her, but Ninik only shrugged that off: "Not much can be done about that. One of us was liable to remind you of him, so it might as well be me."

It was in the same cypress grove where she had loved spending time as a child that Ninik first kissed Zhamants Khoren, the great-grandson of the very Vaghinak whose love was rejected by her great-grandmother Anahit. The grove became the setting of their brief, fleeting encounters: her mother, having lost control over her older daughters, poured all her selfish and suffocating attachment upon her youngest, following her every step and closely monitoring her comings and goings. By then Ninik had completed her nursing degree and found a job at the clinic, and her mother was jealous and threw fits, complaining about being abandoned every time Ninik got held up at work. That is why Ninik and Khoren had to meet in the cypress grove, and her mother, who remembered her childhood habit of spending time there, let her go, unconcerned. The only time Ninik dared to show some gumption and went against her mother's wishes was when she decided to get married. After long quarrels, her mother gave in, making Ninik promise that they would live with her. She tolerated her son-in-law's presence with gritted teeth, responding to all questions with cold silence and leaving the room without even looking his way every time he entered. Khoren treated her enmity with humor, ironically calling her "Mommy," asked her questions, and did everything he could for her without waiting for her to respond. Ninik sometimes laughed and sometimes scolded him, but inwardly she knew that if anyone could handle her mother, that person could only be the new man of their family. Ninik wasn't the only person who understood this—so did her mother, which was why she never yielded any ground to her son-in-law and never would.

The war broke out right after they celebrated their first wedding anniversary, and it took Khoren almost right away. Ninik still froze in unbearable pain every time she recalled how, frightened by a loud knock (nobody ever knocked in Berd—people would just open the door and call out), she came out into the hallway already knowing that something terrible had happened. The triumphant sound of her mother's voice still reverberated in her ears: "It wasn't for naught that I tried to talk you out of marrying him. I could feel in my heart that nothing good would come of it."

"Will you shut up for once!" Ninik snapped back and pushed past her, intentionally brushing against her with her shoulder. She stumbled and fell but managed to contort her body to protect her round belly, then crawled, propelling herself with her hands, and pressed her head against the corner of the sofa and fell silent.

Her daughter was born with the arrival of spring—a pretty, big-eyed girl with dark hair and dimples on her cheeks. Ninik gave her a made-up name, Khoreni, in memory of her father; Ninik's mother scoffed and persisted in calling the girl her own preferred way, but she adored her and completely took over her care. Ninik's work forced her to be absent for days on end; there were so many wounded soldiers in the hastily put together military hospital that she often stayed there around the clock. The girl was quiet and kind, and by two months she was already full of baby talk, recognizing her grandmother and greeting her with her whole body: she bent forward and stretched her plump hands and legs toward her. Once, having fed and swaddled her, her grandmother put her down for a nap and decided to pay her neighbor a quick visit. By the time she returned, the baby was no longer breathing: she had choked on her own spit-up.

Ninik reached the remote room when Zhamants Vaghinak's clock, coughing heavily, struck eight. Her mother was lying down, her eyes covered with the crook of her elbow. When she heard the door creak, she moved her hands and raised herself. Ninik put down the breakfast tray, kissed her mother on the forehead and on her eyes. She threw the shutters wide and opened the window to let in the fresh morning air. While she was fetching water for the morning wash, her mother cried as usual, quietly, without sobs and lamentations. Ninik carried an enameled basin filled with warm water into the room, wetted a towel, thoroughly wrung it out, undressed her mother, and wiped her emaciated, transparent body clean. She put a fresh nightgown on her and tossed the old one under the bed to wash later. She helped her mother sit up, arranging her head pillows in such a way that she could lean against them. She started feeding her like a baby, carefully collecting with the side of the spoon the droplets of porridge that trickled out from the corners of her mouth. She slathered soft cheese on a slice of bread and dipped it in honey, but her mother shook her head no: she was full. Ninik brushed the crumbs off her nightgown, poured some fresh water into a glass, and positioned it within her mother's reach. She left the carafe, with the old silver coin glistening at the bottom, on the bedside table. She walked out, carefully shutting the door behind her. For lunch she would cook a country chicken soup with rice and egg yolk, generously seasoned with chopped cilantro, her mother's favorite. For supper Ninik would bake *sali*: thin puff pastry sprinkled with sugar. She had to get started on the pastry right away because it was labor-intensive.

First she put the chicken on to boil, then mixed the dough, covered it with a towel, and set it aside to rest. While she was mixing the melted butter and flour for the crumbly filling, in

a remote room of the house with a view of the cypress grove,
her mother lay quietly crying. Since the day the baby girl died,
Ninik hadn't spoken a single word to her. She never reproached
or accused her. Debilitated by grief, she still took care of
her, loyally and lovingly. She carried her pain with wordless,
humble dignity. And she remained silent, silent.

Laughter

"Look at how deep the wind has gotten into you!" old Ehizabet tut-tutted in frustration, wrapping up her grandson in the thickest blanket made of itchy sheep wool. Suro's teeth clattered; he blew on his frozen fingers, pulled his feet up to his stomach, and dug his head into the pillow, but he still could not get warm. Ehizabet checked his forehead with her palm and sighed with relief—no fever. Then she helped him pull thick woolen socks on his icy feet, threw a second blanket over the first one, and carefully tucked in the edges.

The blazing stove was crackling, throwing the flame's shimmering light upon the floor. Ehizabet opened the furnace flap, raked up the burning logs with the poker to clear some space, and put two bricks inside. She pulled a faded sheet out of the linen chest, tore it in half, and then tore each half into several pieces. With the poker, she pulled out the hot bricks, wrapped them in the rags, and put them at her grandson's feet. He pressed his feet tightly against the stones and sniffed, inhaling the familiar smell of the heated starched cloth.

"*Tsavd tanem*, Suro-jan," Ehizabet whispered, again tucking in the blanket. "Lie still while I make you a medicinal brew."

She put a fistful of thyme and mint into the kettle and poured some boiling water over it. After letting it steep, she

added three tablespoons of dogwood berry jam. She strained
the drink into a cup. She positioned herself on the edge of
the daybed and carefully pulled back the blanket. Suro raised
himself on his elbow, reaching with his lips for the cup, and
swallowed greedily, scalding his mouth. He fidgeted, changing
his body's position because the empty shirtsleeve, twisted into
a knot and stuck under his side, was bothering him. Ehizabet
pulled out the sleeve and straightened it out.

"It would be better if you just cut it off and use it for a rag,"
Suro snapped irritably. "It is just flopping around aimlessly
anyway!"

She rebuked him with annoyance: "*Bala-jan,*[1] have you
thought this through before saying such things?"

He scoffed, falling quiet. He took away the cup, awkwardly
picking it up with his crippled index finger; she handed it over
without resistance, but not without protectively sliding her
hand under the cup.

"I won't spill it, I am not a child," Suro mumbled, but not
angrily. Ehizabet didn't argue, nor did she remove her palm.

"Feeling warmer?" she asked, smoothing out his disheveled
hair. He wanted to move away but didn't, so as not to upset her.

"I'm all warm."

"Where did you get stuck for so long?"

"In Chinari. We got caught in a shooting. We had to drive
with blown-out windows. Thankfully, there wasn't much damage
to the car: we just need to restore the fender and obviously put
in a new windshield and side window. They shoot generously,
but aimlessly; they're just as bad at fighting now as before."

"That's why you're frozen to the bones—the wind was
blowing into your faces the whole time!" Ehizabet shook her

---

1 "Dear child" (colloquial Armenian).

head, ignoring her grandson's caustic comment about the enemy's military prowess.

Suro returned the cup to her and made an adorable grimace: "*Vay, babo, vay!*"[2]

"Now he is laughing! Come on, cover yourself. Should I prepare a hot bath so that you can get steamed through and chase the illness away?"

"Let me just rest for now, maybe later."

He buried his head in his pillow and pressed his feet against the bricks; they had cooled off a little but still radiated warmth, spreading comforting dry heat over his veins. Ehizabet stood up with a groan and went to rinse out the cup.

"Just don't throw out the dogwood berries," he yelled after her.

"I might be old, but I'm not so senile as to forget that you like tea-soaked berries!"

The wooden shed that served as the utility room was located right under the stairs leading to the veranda. They used to wash dishes in the kitchen, but the war changed everything: their house stood on the very edge of town and could be easily seen from the enemy side. So snipers entertained themselves catching Ehizabet's silhouette in the windows. They shattered all her windows and broke all her dishes. The men of Berd hurriedly put together some shutters and fitted them over the gaping window frames, but the shooting didn't stop, and the bullets effortlessly penetrated the wooden covers. She had to move to the northern part of the house and build an addition for the kitchen under the veranda stairs.

The water was freezing cold, but Ehizabet did not bother with fetching hot water: cold water would do just fine for rinsing a cup. She stood on tiptoe, removed the metal cover

---

2 Ironic: "Woe is me, grandma!"

from the water heater, and looked to check the water level. It would last the day, but she had to top it up in the morning. After washing the cup, she for some reason did not put it back on the handy shelf in the cupboard (the shelf held all her regularly used dishes and was therefore positioned at such a height that she could easily reach all its corners) but instead turned it around in her hands and tucked it in the pocket of her apron.

She checked on Suro: he was sleeping, his mouth open.

"That's good," Ehizabet thought with satisfaction: a deep sleep always benefited her grandson; since early childhood he had always had an amazing ability to overcome his colds by sleeping them away. Cracking the window just wide enough to air out the stove heat, she retired to her room.

The phone stood on the nightstand next to the old television set. Ehizabet carefully carried it, holding up the wire in order not to step on it by accident. Setting the phone down on the windowsill, she returned for a chair. She positioned it to have her left side facing the window. She reached into her pocket for her glasses, discovered the teacup, and called herself a forgetful sheep. Having placed her glasses on the bridge of her nose, she began to press the telephone buttons with an aura of self-importance, marveling yet again over how easy it had become to dial a number. Before, with the rotary phone, it would take half a day to dial, but now one-two-three, and there it was. After several beeps, she heard the scratchy voice of Makarants Tehmine, who, in some miraculous way, always knew who was calling her.

"Is that you, Ehizabet?" she guessed correctly yet again.

"How did you know it was me?" Ehizabet marveled.

Tehmine laughed. "I could sense it. How is Suro?"

"He is sleeping. How is your Kolik?"

"He took the car in for repairs. All the windows are broken except the rear one. There are some bullet holes on the right. They were aiming at the tires but missed."

A tense silence followed. Ehizabet swallowed her tears. It was beyond their strength to talk about what would have happened to their grandsons if even one bullet had hit the tires. Zakinants Martiros had just returned from captivity. He was in such a state that his daughter fainted when she saw his injuries.

"I wish they could build a safe road, one that didn't run along the border," Tehmine sighed.

"Don't hold your breath. They would rather choke on that money than build anything," Ehizabet retorted bitterly, meaning the government, which had been feeding people empty promises for several years now.

Tehmine's heavy sighs could be heard through the humming of the phone wires. "That's all right," she finally responded, "everyone will get what they deserve. Everyone."

Ehizabet made a rapid gesture with her hand as if chasing away an annoying fly. She clipped the cup, which fell off the window, hit the floor with a dull thud, and split in half.

"I don't believe in justice, Tehmo! And I don't believe in retribution. Why did my Suro have to suffer? He lost his family in the bombing and lives a cripple, with one hand torn off by the explosion, the other mangled. You've seen for yourself how he sorts through the greens with his deformed fingers, how hard he works to feed himself and me. Or your poor Kolik? First he buried his wife, then his oldest daughter. Now he's forced to drive to the city on this cursed road under constant shelling to buy shoe repair supplies. Why does he have to suffer? Or poor Arto, who is still mourning his Zabel? I once dropped a hint: I said, 'Why bury yourself alive? Ask for

Ninik's hand in marriage, she is a nice girl, you can get married while you are still young, you'll have children, you'll be happy together.' But he just waved his hand: 'What children can there be if your heart is shot through with pain?' You tell me: Why do our children and grandchildren suffer? And for what holy deeds do those jerks in power deserve to get fat?"

"Pick those words more carefully, Ehizo," Tehmine said anxiously.

"Why is that?"

"Who knows, maybe those in power won't like these words very much."

"I shit on their heads!" Ehizabet exclaimed in desperation and anger. "They won't like my words, is that it? I shit on their heads every morning. And every evening! Got it?"

"I get it, what's not to get," Tehmine responded serenely.

Ehizabet slammed the phone receiver on the windowsill, bent down, picked up the cup's shards, and put them into her apron pocket. Then she lifted the receiver back to her ear.

"Oh yes? What exactly do you get?" she asked, catching her breath.

"I understand that you go to the bathroom for number two like you go to work, every morning. But if you get angry, you may also go in the evening."

They laughed, wiping the tears with the edges of their sleeves. Ehizabet, sitting near the window of her house on the shelled outskirts of Berd; Tehmine, in the hallway of her house, which, although safe from sniper bullets because it was located on the other side of town, frequently got caught in mortar fire, for those places that bullets didn't reach were unfailingly found by explosives.

Immortelle

"Chee-yaaa, chee-yaaa," reverberated the annoying hullabaloo of the motley guinea fowl. They wandered, wobbling, through the potato bushes, looking for striped beetles. Unlike other farm birds, they didn't dig up garden beds, which is why Ashkhen allowed them into the orchard unhindered, although she still tried to keep an eye on them: they may be harmless for garden beds, but they can peck the sprouts so much that later she would have to turn to her neighbor Vardanush for help. As if reading her thoughts, Vardanush—a sturdy woman of unimposing stature with an unhealthy redness on her flabby cheeks—materialized in the opening of the fence. Sizing up Ashkhen with her tenacious, dull-blue eyes and without returning her greeting, she continued to sweep her yard. Ashkhen shrugged her shoulders but did not call out her neighbor for her rudeness: What's the point of explaining such simple things to an adult? In Berd, it was customary to return a greeting with "May God bless your day," and if Vardanush has nothing to say even to her creator, why should a mere mortal be upset?

Her neighbor took her time scratching the dry surface of the yard with her broom and raising clouds of dust. "She was too lazy to sprinkle the ground with water, so now she is swallowing dirt," Ashkhen sighed and turned her attention to the fowl scurrying around the potatoes. Two of the birds had reached the sprouts of savory and were busy plucking the tender leaves, constantly clattering. "What silly birds," thought Ashkhen sluggishly, but she did not chase them away: she no longer had anyone who would eat fresh savory, and she had enough of it dried in the cellar to last her three lifetimes. As soon as her father's grave is put in order, she will plant savory all around the headstone. It will grow and bloom, smelling piquant-spicy in hot weather and tangy-fresh on cloudy days. Let him rest comfortably.

On the stone floor of the veranda, the stalks of the lilac-colored immortelle lay drying, bathed in the morning light. Her father could not stand the modern plastic brooms and was also apprehensive about sorghum ones: it was not native to Berd, so why use it? He gathered immortelle the old-fashioned way, meticulously sorted it, and tied it into brooms, all of which came out like dressy girls from the North: long, fair-haired, with faded flowers woven into their braids. You walked over your freshly swept yard, and it was as if you were treading over a field baked crisp by the August sun. Wet one of these brooms, and it smelled of everything you inhaled since your childhood: moist floorboards, sour plums, sorrel crushed between your fingers, barely fermented wine . . . Ah!

Ashkhen rose, carefully folded the shawl in which she had wrapped herself despite the clear morning, and draped it over the veranda banister, taking care that it didn't cast a shadow over the drying immortelle stalks. She reshuffled them, turning every stem over to make sure it dried evenly on all sides. She could get started on them by the week's end. Of course, she could never do as fine a job as her father did: the people of Berd would say, tut-tutting their tongues in awe, that his every broom was a piece of art fit for a museum. But she will try her best: after all, she had watched him doing it since childhood. She will leave one broom for herself and take the other one to the cemetery. She has to ask Mayinants Tsatur if she can keep it in his shed; otherwise, if she leaves it out in the open, it may get damaged by wind or rain. Once they install a fence around the grave and clear the path leading to the headstone, Ashkhen will use this broom to keep everything tidy. Just yesterday she stopped at the stonemason's to see how things were progressing. Her father would have liked his headstone. It was a black slab, elongated at the top, with the dates of his birth and death and with his name: Martiros Kojoyan. Ashkhen turned down the idea of putting his portrait on it—she had never managed to have a new picture taken, and didn't want to use the one that was printed in the newspaper because her father looked so awful in it that her heart shrank with pain. He had looked completely different her whole life, but she would remember him only like that—an old broken man who jumped at the slightest sound, dying in agony.

"Who is it?" he would exclaim every time he heard steps behind him, and he'd throw himself on the ground and hide his face in his hands.

At first, she tried to comfort him and tried to get him to stand up, but he wouldn't budge; he only shouted and wailed, pressing himself deeper into the floor. Then she started covering his body with hers, protecting him, as if from shelling.

"Daddy, it's me, your Ashkhen," she would repeat over and over, feeling his body relax little by little. He'd stay quiet for a long time, but then, retreating from his nightmare, he would start whispering again and again, like a prayer: "Dear Lord, I am home. And this is my daughter. Dear Lord, I am home. And this is my daughter."

He would find and grab her hand, press it to his lips.

"How are you doing?" she would ask.

"I am all right, *tsavd tanem.*"

If it were possible to die of grief, Ashkhen would have died right then and there. She lay on top of her father, embracing his shoulders with her arms and, restraining her own sobs, frantically breathed in his scent. During his time in captivity, he had become emaciated and smelled of loneliness and despair. She stroked his neck, his head, completely shaved and peppered with tattoos; some of them were covered with scabs that wouldn't heal but the drawings were still distinguishable: a half-moon with a star, an eastern scroll. What must happen to people's souls and to what extent must they lose respect for themselves, their God, and their elderly parents to do such things to a seventy-year-old man? Ashkhen asked herself, and she failed to find an answer.

Her father burned rapidly, almost immediately after he was returned. His demise was agonizing and labored: he suffered from panic attacks and horrific pain, struggled for breath, drifted in and out of consciousness, and bled profusely.

"Do something!" Ashkhen would cry in frustration. The doctors only shrugged helplessly: before her father was handed over to the Red Cross, which was involved in negotiating the return of prisoners of war, they had injected him with forbidden substances against which medical intervention was powerless.

"Do something!" Ashkhen demanded from the investigator. He continued to chain-smoke.

"We did everything we could: we started an investigation into kidnapping and torture," he frowned, frustrated by the meaninglessness of his own answer, and averted his eyes.

"But someone needs to get justice!" Ashkhen persisted.

"Who, if not you?" The investigator would finish his cigarette in two puffs and keep silent. Once, during one of her visits, he pulled out of his safe a thick stack of folders and put it in front of her. He sat opposite her and folded his hands, one of them for some reason palm up, as if inviting her to put her hand on top of it. She looked at his palm for a couple of seconds, absent-mindedly registering the broken lifeline, frowned, chasing away the irrelevant thoughts, opened the top folder, and, upon noticing Krnatants Antaram's name, bit her lip.

"That's justice for you," said the investigator with a bitter smirk. "We've appealed to all kinds of international organizations. Nobody cares about us."

"So, what am I supposed to do now?" she asked.

The investigator shrugged his shoulders and looked away.

Ashkhen never went back to his office.

"They tortured me so much, daughter," her father would complain when he could no longer stand his suffering. "What didn't they do to me!"

"What . . . did they do?" she would echo, frozen with horror.

Her father died at sunset, just as Ashkhen stopped by his room to make sure that he was sleeping. He was nearing the end, expiring in agony, suffocating, clinging to the weightless air with his fingers, his hollow eyes looking on dreadfully and darkly. His bedding was completely soaked in the blood that was seeping from all of his pores, blanketing with a sticky veil his body, tortured by poison and emaciated beyond recognition.

The first thing Ashkhen did after the funeral was to go to the field where her father used to gather the immortelle. She spread her shawl and lay down, spreading her arms. It was so quiet and tranquil all around, as if an entire cartload of peace had been poured over the world. Up high, dense, snow-white clouds were floating by, rapidly changing their outlines. "Bad weather must be coming if the heavenly shepherd is hurrying his flock," Ashkhen thought, and dissolved into bitter sobs. On that ill-fated morning, preparing to gather immortelle, her father had said the same things as he watched the turmoil in the sky. He had taken an unusually long time to get ready, getting distracted with one thing or another. Ashkhen even reproached him: the day has passed, it's noon already, it will start raining soon, and you are procrastinating. Her father guiltily mumbled some excuses and went out, forgetting to take his lunch. She found the package with sandwiches on the bench under the mulberry tree and got upset, but then talked herself down—I will ask Masis, he's a good kid, he won't refuse. Masis did not refuse, of course, but he also didn't find anyone in the immortelle field. Sensing that something was wrong, she went to the soldiers and they combed the neighboring area all the way to the neutral territory but came up empty-handed. After several weeks they received word that her father had been taken prisoner.

From the day he passed away, Ashkhen lost her ability to take full breaths. Her relatives tried to convince her to seek medical help, but she waved them off: there is nothing to worry about, my health will take care of itself. She went on living like she did before, taking care of her children and waiting for her husband, who spent half of every month on the border. Sometimes, when she was clipping the wings of a particularly boisterous guinea fowl to prevent it from flying away, she would think that she herself had turned into such a fowl, pinned to the ground by grief and by the impossibility to overcome it. Despite her deep despair, her thoughts about her father were airy and bright. In those shiny places where his soul had found an abode, there would definitely be a field where he could gather immortelle without any fear of being kidnapped and tortured to death. Ashkhen was certain of that. The skies are endless immortelle fields, lilac-blue and vast. Now her father knows that for sure.

Guilt

H aving rumbled with thunder, the sky wiped off
the clouds and, by midday, sparkled with a freshly
washed blue. Vardanush opened the shutters of her
shushaband, momentarily letting the delicate chiming of the air
into her house. The feisty mountain wind was traveling beyond
the horizon, dragging the torn skirt of the thinning rain with
it. "Chee-yaaa, chee-yaaa," screeched her neighbor Ashkhen's
guinea fowl behind the fence, delighted by the change in the
weather, and their senseless clucking filled Vardanush with
dull but mounting annoyance. "May the plague take you
all!" Vardanush wished them with bile, and angrily shut the
windows. She pulled the sun-bleached blinds tightly to make
sure no light got through because even as a child, she had hated
seeing the slanted streaks of sunshine on the floor. Then she
slowly and pensively walked through the house, inspecting it
with such genuine curiosity it would seem she was seeing it
for the first time. In the hallway, she looked over the wooden
daybed critically, fluffed up the pillows, arranged them in
a neat row along the wall, and then took two steps back to
admire their beauty. The autumn of the previous year, when she
had some free time, she had embroidered daisies and poppies
on them, and now the pillows warmed her soul and cheered

her eyes with their bright colors. Along the edges of the daybed she positioned full-bodied velvet *mutakas*[1] stuffed taut with felt rags; these royal viziers, haughty and obdurate, were the heirs of centuries of Persian rule that had left an indelible mark on the households of many Eastern Armenian families. Using her forefinger, Vardanush evened out the tips of their silver-threaded ties. She cast one last critical glance over the daybed and, satisfied with its appearance, moved on.

The dining room was cool and very dark, with abandoned cobwebs covering one corner of the ceiling. An old wind-up clock stood on the bookcase, facing the entrance with its dull face. Judging by the time it showed, it had stopped only a few minutes earlier. Getting on her tiptoes and groaning from the effort, Vardanush hurriedly wound up the clock again, turning the spring almost all the way, but she did not reset the hands—she had no need to because she had a remarkable, unerring sense of time. She needed the clock not for keeping track of time but for another reason: its loud and demanding ticktock provided some much-needed noise in the otherwise resounding silence of her house. Despite her lasting, perpetual solitude, Vardanush feared death and hoped to live as long as possible. This was why she wound up the clock, firmly believing that life went on for as long as its course was measured.

She didn't peek into her son's bedroom; there was nothing for her to do there and nothing to see. It was an unremarkable room—a dresser topped with an oval mirror with whitish speckles, a bed covered neatly with a woolen blanket, and a closet, completely empty save for a folded cotton robe on the top shelf, left behind by Vardanush's daughter-in-law.

---

1 Of Persian origin, the word *mutaka* is used in Armenian to mean oblong, large, stiff pillows for couches.

Vardanush had considered returning it but changed her mind every time: her daughter-in-law would have sent someone for it a long time ago if she had needed it. If she hadn't, that's how it was meant to be.

Nor did she inspect her own room—as it was, she was condemned to spending endless nights there, sighing, grumbling, tossing from side to side and waiting for sleep to come. She normally nodded off only as the sleepy sky already began extinguishing the dimming light of its stars. From then until the first honking of the passing garbage truck, she would fall into a brief reverie, sinking into it as if into a dark and bottomless abyss. She never had any dreams or at least didn't remember them, and was frankly relieved about this because her grandma, God rest her soul, had always insisted that dreams were reflections of how other people felt about someone, so whatever others thought of a person, that would be the kind of dreams that person would have. Not that Vardanush really believed her grandma's words, but, considering the general hostility that the people of Berd felt toward her, she drew comfort in her dreamless slumber.

"The last thing I need is for them to get to me at night too," she'd mumble to herself, scraping the dry ground with a broom and embracing the dull annoyance that washed over her every time she thought of her fellow townspeople. They would notice a straw in someone else's eyes but miss a log in their own! Even Ashkhen! Just today, she was clearly judging Vardanush, thinking that she had gotten too lazy to sprinkle some water over her dried-up yard. Or, even worse, she was probably thinking that Vardanush was doing it on purpose to suffocate her neighbors with dust. But what point was there in watering the yard, she'd like to know, if it was about to start raining anyway? The clear sky couldn't fool Vardanush; she felt the arrival of inclement weather in her body: it ached and throbbed, reverberating in every bone, and her head hurt as if it had split open, so badly that it made her want to lie down and die on the spot. But could you confide all of this to your neighbor who had no interest in your explanations, because she had long ago decided that she knew everything there was to know about you? And she says hello, mind you, even smiles! What a hypocritical bunch of people they are: they say one thing to your face and think the opposite behind your back! It would have been better if they just walked past and ignored her—she had done just fine without them for fifteen years, and she could go on like this forever!

For all her bellicose intractability, Vardanush nevertheless found solitude oppressive. When she could no longer stand it, she would pay a visit to Hovinants Mariam, the only person with whom she was on cordial terms. Mariam would make her mint tea and offer some simple treats. While Vardanush vented, Mariam knitted or embroidered—she was not used to being idle. Having gotten everything off her chest, Vardanush would start saying goodbye, never having touched her tea.

"Maybe I'll stop by again later?" she would ask, indecisively shuffling her feet by the door.

Mariam would stand frozen in her tracks for a second, as if not understanding what was expected of her, before clasping her hands: "Vardanush-moqir, why do you ask? You are welcome here any time you like. I am always happy to see you."

"Thank you, child."

IN THE PHOTO ALBUM of her son's school years, a large black-and-white photograph sat prominently displayed on the very first page, its corners tucked neatly into the incisions in the cardboard: he and Mariam in first grade, looking dazed, seated behind the desk, with their hands awkwardly folded in front of them. On the picture, Mariam's hair is plaited into two thin braids and tied with enormous bows. Her son's shirt collar is folded. To this day, Vardanush runs her fingers over it, as if trying to straighten the unruly fabric. His eyes are large, slightly bulging, his eyebrows bleached so blond by the sun that they're invisible on the photo. They were bleached but thick in an unchildlike way. Practically since his birth, Vardanush kept trying to smooth and shape them with her spit-wetted fingertip. He would make faces and try to break free—he didn't like being touched.

Vardanush raised him all by herself. Her husband, who had left to make money in the North, found himself another wife there. At first, he called once in a while and sent them some money, but eventually he cut off contact altogether. She had been anticipating this, because she knew that most men, once they rejected one family in favor of another, invariably severed all the threads connecting them to their past in order to silence their nagging conscience. The moment her husband vanished from her life forever, Vardanush collected every single item in the house that reminded her of him, piled everything in the yard, and set it on fire. Her son was only three at the time and, oblivious to what was happening, was delighted by the bonfire. He ran around it in circles, tossing in a twig here, a blade of grass there. Vardanush didn't try to stop him as she watched, with frank satisfaction, how the fire consumed the items one by one: her husband's favorite guitar, his books, his double-breasted tweed blazer for which they had saved up for a long time by setting money aside from their measly salaries, the snow-white cotton dress shirt with tiny blue boats on the cuffs that Vardanush had embroidered for him in a single night. Her husband had worn that shirt with pride and left it behind

when he went up North because he was afraid he would get it
stained. He kept promising her: "As soon as I come back, I'll
put on that shirt and we will go to the movies and watch your
favorite: *Three Poplars in Plyushchikha*."[2] He never returned; they
never went anywhere together again.

Growing up, her son was a difficult child. He insisted on
doing everything on his own terms, often just to antagonize
his mother. He completed his military service and went to
university to study agronomy. He took a wife without asking
for his mother's blessing, a poorly educated girl who had
completed only eight years of school[3] and worked providing
child care at a local nursery. Vardanush disapproved of his
choice, but there was nothing she could do—not like she
could've just kicked out the young couple to live in the streets.
She did not argue with her son because her love for him was
too great, but, sensing her own power, she went out of her
way to torment her daughter-in-law, a quiet and obedient
homegrown girl, with caustic, critical remarks—you under-
starched the sheets and didn't iron them properly; your bread
is rock-hard because you overknead the dough; you leave dirty
smudges on the floors when washing them. "Where do you see
smudges? Show me!" her son once snapped at her, no longer
able to contain himself. "I see them where I need to," Vardanush retorted. Her daughter-in-law was silently wiping her
eyes. Everything in her posture, from her bowed head to her
fingers frantically tugging at the edge of her sleeve, bespoke
her boundless misery. Vardanush felt a prickle of conscience
and stopped short; for a brief stretch of time she even left
the girl alone, but eventually she went back to harassing her

2 A hugely popular 1968 Soviet feature film directed by Tatiana Lioznova.

3 At the time, primary and secondary education in Armenia was ten years, but only
eight years were mandatory.

with redoubled zeal, taking out on her all the bile she had accumulated during her long years of womanly loneliness.

The war took her son during the bitter freezes of February. Once she buried him, Vardanush, firmly convinced that she was doing the right thing, took her pregnant daughter-in-law to get an abortion. At five and a half months, she was too far along, but Vardanush found an amenable doctor and got her way for a formidable sum of money. The daughter-in-law, made helpless by her grief, submitted without a word. As soon as she was discharged from the hospital, she gathered her belongings and returned to her family.

From that day on, the people of Berd turned their backs on Vardanush. She, for her part, considered it beneath her to owe them any explanation and went on to cut off any communication with them without regret. She lived burdened by her loneliness but also in some way having grown fond of it. She never allowed herself to shed tears for her son and rarely visited his grave. When a rowdy bunch of kids ran past her yard on their way to the river, she would straighten up, shield her eyes from the blinding sun with the palm of her hand, and search among them for her former daughter-in-law's sons, born less than a year apart. She mouthed to herself—here's one, and there's the other. Time passed, the daughter-in-law remarried and had children, but Vardanush still remembered the day when she, pale, with dark circles under her eyes, had packed her things, trying to be as quiet as possible and periodically placing a palm on her bulging midsection out of habit before quickly pulling it away, as if afraid. She left, leaving on top of the dresser the only valuable thing she had—her wedding band. Vardanush called after her, but she didn't look back. Whether she heard Vardanush or not, God only knows.

Salvation

Every mother-in-law in Berd likes to say: Hovinants Mariam is the best, one of a kind. She does her laundry to a fault: she adds just enough bluing detergent, just enough starch, and never overdries the sheets. She irons them with a heavy coal iron, folds them into neat stacks, and never forgets to layer them with small chintz bags filled with dried wild lavender. When you lift the lid of her bedding chest, it exudes such pristine cleanliness that you feel awkward just looking at it, let alone being in its proximity.

Mariam darns so well that you can't make out the stitches on the fabric. She washes the windows in three waters—first with soap, then regular, then diluted with wine vinegar. She polishes the floors with beeswax to the point that they sparkle like puddles on a moonlit night. Her yard is always swept clean; in the shed, her firewood is stacked in rows as neat as honeycomb cells; the paths in her vegetable garden are laid with river gravel. Who in all of Berd cares about the look of their garden paths? Only Mariam!

She cooks so well that you eat and eat and can't stop. Her bread is so airy it seems as if it were made of ethereal sunlight instead of flour; her canned vegetables smell of summer;

her *gata*, which she keeps in the cooling oven to give it its inimitably delicate crust, melts in your mouth.

"If you want to be a real homemaker, try to be more like Hovinants Mariam," women all over Berd keep saying to their daughters-in-law. The daughters-in-law feel slightly offended, but they don't grumble, for who would dare say a word against Mariam? She is the best, one of a kind, and the other women know this for sure.

Mariam used to have a large family: a husband, a few sons, aging parents-in-law, and an ancient grandmother. There was a time when she had everything: a brick house, a garden with paths so well kept that her mother-in-law would show them off to their neighbors. Once, she also had a peach orchard right by the border, at the mouth of a raucous mountain river. That year, the harvest was the most bountiful they had ever had, and the entire family went to pick peaches while Mariam stayed back to cook syrup for her peach jam. Who could have thought that war breaks out so suddenly and so stealthily? Who could have known?

They didn't win back control of the borderland until the end of winter. The soldiers buried the mangled human remains right in the peach orchard. Mariam made her way there, lay down on the burial mound, and didn't rise. They found her the next morning, frozen to the bone, with iced-over eyelashes and blue lips. It took a long time to nurse her back to life. By then, the enemy had once again won control of the orchard, and it remained on the other side of the border forever.

Each of Mariam's days resembles all the others, like the stones in her ancient grandmother's prayer beads: sweep the yard, water the garden, light the stove, make the dough, bake the bread. She does everything meticulously, with care; she washes her windows in three waters, she carefully starches and irons the sheets, never forgetting to layer them with dried lavender to keep off the all-pervading moths.

All people have their own truths. Mariam's is as simple as it gets: no matter how badly your soul aches and no matter how much your heart weeps, you must maintain order in the one tiny sliver of the world that has been entrusted to you. After all, that's all you can do for its salvation.

Fogs

Pashoiants Sona draws the fogs of her childhood. In Berd, they are different: impenetrable and dense, they plunge down the mountains like rivers of milk, rushing onward and onward, toward the courtyards, gates, and defenseless *shushabands*. It seems like with one push of a shoulder the glass will shatter into pieces, and then the fog will make its way into the houses and melt them without a trace: there was Berd, and—poof—it is gone.

Pashoiants Sona draws the fogs of her childhood. In her drawings, the fogs smell of loneliness and longing. They don't simply distort the space but change its very essence—just yesterday, one could reach the neighbor's house in a single breath, but now it feels like it will take an eternity. The fogs in Berd care not about time—they exist in a dimension where time doesn't exist.

Pashoiants Sona has a large family: a mother, a father, three older sisters, and a little brother. Her mother teaches Russian language and literature at school, and her father is a doctor. When the fighting peaks, he has to travel to the hospital during shelling, and nobody knows whether or not he has reached it because there is no way to call and ask—the phones are silent.

The stone school building is long gone—all schooling takes place in dank military tents. They have neither electricity nor heating. It gets so cold in the winter that the children write without removing their gloves. Then Sona's mother stays up late deciphering their scribbles because gloves greatly distort one's handwriting. Recently she has been spending long days at school, preparing a special lesson about Byron and rehearsing a performance with her upperclassmen.

"Why? Why are you doing this?" Sona once asked in despair.

"One has to live," her mother responded evenly.

And so they live. They sleep in the hallway, which is the safest room of the house. The father positions himself near the door so that in case of an air raid he can rush to the hospital right away. The older sisters take the outer edges of the mattresses arranged on the floor, leaving the spaces in the middle for their younger siblings. The brother is very little, only four years old. During shelling, he hides his face in his hands. "Maybe you should plug your ears instead? The noise is scarier," his sisters try to talk some sense into him. The brother hides his face in his hands and remains silent.

Sona knows plenty of things about war that it would have been better not to know: that before going to bed, you have to lock all the doors, and the ones with glass paneling you also have to hang with blankets so nobody gets hurt if the glass shatters. That you shouldn't ask for bread if there isn't any—you won't satisfy your hunger anyway, but you will reduce your mother to tears yet again. That you can't complain about the brutal cold because there are significantly worse things out there. And that you mustn't cry when frightened because it only makes everything scarier. Live, as if in a fog, and don't complain.

Sometimes there are short-lived lulls, and every time, people naively think these moments will last forever. And how can they feel otherwise, if at dawn the roosters break into carefree song, followed by the cicadas at noon, and then the crickets at sunset. There are so many stars at night that you think someone has laid Christmas lights over the dome of heaven and deliberately left them on. Sona is lying in her bed—what bliss it is to lie not on the floor in the hallway but in her own bed!—and watching the enormous lunar orb glide through the sky. Grandma used to tell her that once upon a time, the moon was a very beautiful but lazy young girl who preferred idly resting on the riverbank to working. Once her mother asked the moon to help out with the bread, but the moon did not even deign to answer because she was too busy admiring her reflection in the river. Upset, her mother threw a piece of dough at her, hitting her in the face. The moon fell into the river, which carried her out into the sky. From then on, as a punishment for her laziness, the moon is forced to shine whenever people are resting. And if you look really hard, you can still make out the imprint of dried dough on the moon's face.

Sona falls asleep way past midnight, when the moon's aggrieved face disappears behind the cornice of the roof. Night is merciful and silent, the stars in the sky are whispering something to each other, the world is lulled to sleep by the crickets' lullaby . . .

An explosion goes off nearby, right outside the house. Sona rushes to the only safe corner of the room. She is lying on her back, her arms wrapped around herself, watching as the charred remains of the curtains circle in the air. They land on her in black ash flakes, and the only thought running through her head is how she can even see them in this impenetrable darkness. From where Sona is lying, she can see Ursa Major's dipper and the white star on its tail.

In the morning the sun peeks out. In its rays, Berd sparkles like Christmas tinsel, shattered glass covering it like a rug. There is so much broken glass, it seems as if under the cover of night all the world's glass was transported here and shattered all at once. Father comes from the hospital only to make sure that everyone is in one piece. He sits down for a minute, takes a breath, and sinks into a deep sleep. Sona caresses his cheek—he hasn't shaved for a while, so his stubble has almost grown into a beard. The older sisters stretch plastic wrap over the windows; it's hard to find glass in the besieged town, and it doesn't even make sense to replace it, since it will all be blown out again during the next air raid.

Pashoiants Sona caresses her sleeping father's cheek with her burned little palm. She is already drawing Berd—an image that will remain with her forever. She will keep drawing it for many long years, whenever the slightest rustle induces a panic attack in her: "postwar syndrome," a doctor will say helplessly. Then she, a healthy, beautiful woman, will find out that she most likely will be unable to have children. "It happens to girls who live through a major shock, and especially those who experienced hunger in their childhood," yet another doctor will shake his head. When she turns down a chance to travel to faraway New York for an exhibition of her works, a different doctor will explain, "Fear of large spaces is one of the consequences of war-related stress."

"What should I do?" Sona will ask the fourth doctor.

"You know how to draw. Try to draw your fear. Perhaps you can manage it that way."

Pashoiants Sona draws Berd: scared children, wounded women, helpless men, enveloped in silent, indifferent fog.

Pashoiants Sona struggles with her fears the only way she can, on her own.

Pashoiants Sona. My baby sister.

In Lieu of an Epilogue

"Life always conquers death," my great-grandmother Tata always said. I was little and didn't quite understand what she meant, so I shrugged and sighed. I thought to myself that it was a game of sorts: the grownups must recite boring and confusing words, and the children must listen, without worrying about their meaning. Then Tata was gone, and my childhood ended with her passing. And then the war happened, along with many other things that I would love to erase from my memory once and for all.

But I failed to do that.

One of the stories in this collection is about my little sister Sona. It is a difficult ordeal to talk about your own family's pain, which is why that story proved to be especially challenging. I was unsure about including it in the book, so I asked Sona's advice. She said that it was not her story at all. Rather, she said, it was a story of a war that we had the misfortune of experiencing. And one must absolutely write about it, in hopes that . . . and here my sister halted midsentence.

"In hopes that what?" I asked her.

"In hopes that all the broken embraces will be restored," she answered hesitantly. To write about a war means almost destroying any hope within yourself. Like staring death in the face while trying not to avert your eyes. Because if you do, you will have betrayed your own self.

I tried my best. I am not sure that I have succeeded.

My family recently experienced an immense joy—my sister finally had a baby boy. The broken embrace was restored, and Tata's words attained their true meaning.

Life is fairer than death, and that's what encapsulates its unbreakable truth.

It is necessary to believe this in order to go on living.

The Author

Narine Abgaryan was born in 1971 in Berd, Armenia, to a doctor and a schoolteacher. Named one of Europe's most exciting authors by the *Guardian*, she is the author of a dozen books, which have collectively sold over 1.35 million copies. Her book *Three Apples Fell from the Sky* won the Leo Tolstoy Yasnaya Polyana Award and an English PEN Award, and has been translated into twenty-seven languages. Her award-winning trilogy about Manunia, a busy and troublesome eleven-year-old, has been made into a TV series. Abgaryan divides her time between Armenia and Germany.

The Translators

Margarit Ordukhanyan, PhD, is a New York–based scholar and translator of poetry and prose from her native Armenian and Russian into English. Ordukhanyan was the Fall 2022 Translator-in-Residence at the University of Iowa's Translation Workshop and a 2023 National Endowment of the Arts Translation Fellow. She is currently a fellow at the Vartan Gregorian Center for Research in the Humanities at the New York Public Library.

Zara Martirosova Torlone, a native of Armenia, is a professor in the classics department at Miami University, Ohio. She received her BA in classical philology from Moscow University and her PhD in classics from Columbia University. She is the author of *Russia and the Classics* (2009), *Latin Love Poetry* (co-authored, 2014), and *Vergil in Russia* (2015), and co-edited *A Handbook to Classical Reception in Eastern and Central Europe* (2017) and *Virgil and His Translators* (2018).